Morsels of Life

Also by RIK LONSDALE

Water and Blood

Links

www.riklonsdale.com

linktr.ee/riklonsdale

Morsels
of Life

Fifty-five short stories for humans

Rik Lonsdale

For JIS,
and all other humans.

CONTENTS

Fairy Gold

HARRY RECOGNISED ONE of "The Little People" when he saw one and he wouldn't look it in the eye. I'll not be taken for a fool, he thought and prepared to stomp away, ignoring the strange phenomenon that he refused to believe existed.

'Harry, don't be leaving me in such a hurry now.' The words rang in his ears like wind chimes, though no sound was made. His feet, unbidden, stopped dead in their tracks, his forward motion upsetting his balance, almost tumbling him to the forest floor. Harry pulled his fleece around himself, zipped it up, and struggled to heave his feet from the ground.

'That'll do you no good, now. Don't you know I'm here to do you a favour, and you being so rude as to not even look me in the eye.' Harry's head began to turn to face the creature. He tried to stop it but turn it did, whether he chose or not. And when he came face to face with the fairy he was mesmerised.

'There now, that's better. I'll not be keeping you too long, but you're just the strapping sort of young man I need right now. I want your muscles to dig my croc of gold for me. But first I'll just climb on your shoulders, there. And now away with us.'

Harry's feet started to move, faster and faster his legs went. 'But where are we going,' he gasped.

'I told you, to dig my croc of gold, at the end of the rainbow there, so come on, no time to lose.' Harry felt his legs running faster than ever before.

It was a long journey, but finally they arrived, and Harry's arms began to pull up the sods and dig in the soil. Eventually his fingers scratched the top of a metal box. Harry pulled the beautifully decorated box from the ground and opened it. The gold shone bright. Avarice replaced the fear in Harry's eyes.

'So, you would like a little of the gold, would you?' Rang the fairy voice in his ear. 'Well, you can carry me and my gold to my castle and you will be rewarded. Away with you.' And Harry set off again. The fairy on his shoulder and the croc of gold under his arm.

The fairy castle poked its turret above the horizon and Harry knew his journey would soon be over. It had been long and exhausting.

'Now for your reward, faithful Harry. You have a choice. You can have a single piece of gold from the croc I have here, or you can help yourself to as much as you can carry from the croc at the other end of the rainbow. Which will you have?'

Both Harry and the fairy knew he would not be happy with a single piece of gold, so off set Harry's legs again.

Eventually Harry found the other end of the rainbow. It was right in the middle of the M25.

You just can't trust those fairies.

A Day at the Races

'You're looking very dapper today, Mr Johnson.'

Johnny Johnson smiled. He was pleased the young woman serving breakfast remembered his name.

'Thanks very much... err...'

'Claire, it's Claire, Mr Johnson.'

'Ah, yes, of course, Claire. Thank you, I like to look the part, you know.'

He was wearing his best tweed jacket with a tweed tie over brown corduroy trousers and polished brown brogues.

'Where is it today then?' said Claire, filling his cup with tea.

'Cheltenham today, beautiful racecourse. Very popular.'

'Cheltenham, fancy that. It sounds posh.'

'Have you ever been racing... er?'

'Claire. No, I've never been, you'll have to take me one day, Mr Johnson.'

'You wouldn't want to go today; it'll be very cold.'

After breakfast Johnny donned his sheepskin coat and trilby hat and headed for the entrance.

'Mr Johnson, would you like coffee before you go?'

Coffee sounded and smelled good. He had time.

'That would be very welcome. It looks a bit chilly out there.'

Johnny took a newspaper from his coat to study form in the racing pages.

'Have you any tips for me?' said Claire, putting a mug of coffee and a plate of biscuits beside him.

Johnny tapped the side of his nose. 'Between you and me, I rather fancy Bombardier Bill in the 2:30. Should romp home.'

He took out a pencil to circle one or two race picks, but it was blunt. I'll just have to remember, he thought. The chair was comfortable, and Johnny relaxed and closed his eyes.

A gentle rocking of his shoulder woke him.

'It's lunchtime, Mr Johnson, there's soup and a sandwich ready.'

'I'll miss the first race,' he said, 'but it's always a novice's race.'

After lunch Johnny again donned his coat and hat. He tried to push the entrance door open, but it wouldn't budge.

'You need to pull it, Mr Johnson,' called Claire.

'Of course, thank you, er… miss,' and Johnny pulled the door open and stepped outside into the cold air.

Johnny walked down the long garden path, past lawns and flower beds, to the wrought iron gate. He pulled it open and stepped on to the pavement. He stared in confusion at the traffic hurtling by, at the people rushing along. The noise crashed into his ears. He didn't hear the 'excuse me' and 'mind out' of people squeezing past.

Someone jostled him. 'Get out of the way, old man,' they called as they rushed on.

Johnny turned and saw the peaceful garden beyond the gate. He needed to get out of this chaos that surrounded him. He walked past the flower beds and lawns. It seemed to be a hotel. He walked into reception.

'Hello Mr Johnson,' said the receptionist, 'how was Cheltenham?'

Johnny paused a moment, looking confused, then remembered his manners and took off his hat.

'Very good, wonderful racecourse you know, bit chilly though.'

'Would you like a nice cup of tea?'

'That would be very kind, thank you, miss…'

'Claire, it's Claire Mr Johnson.'

Moving Gardens

IT WAS DIFFICULT to leave, but Barbara had no choice. The removal van was laden with their furniture, the car packed with the essentials of kettle, tea and emergency rations. Dennis was waiting, but she had to take a last walk around the garden.

The garden was a history of their time together in the house. The Bramley at the bottom, planted when they first moved in, towered above the fences, sheds, and lesser trees of neighbouring gardens. The two lilacs, commemorating the births of their children, were as strong, sturdy, and mature as Barbara's own son and daughter. She paused at each commemorative plant, remembering why it had been planted. She remembered trips to the garden centre with her children to choose markers for the pets they once had. Bernie, the Dachshund, Frodo, the tortoiseshell, hamsters, guinea pigs, all had a special shrub.

The rose garden, started when grandchildren began to arrive, now had five rose bushes. Barbara smelled each one in turn for what would be the last time.

Dennis came up behind her and gave a quiet cough. He knew how difficult it was to leave their home of forty-two years, but they could no longer manage the large garden and rather than see it overgrown they had sold the house.

'Oh! Dennis, I'm going to miss this so much,' said Barbara, brushing away a tear.

'I will too, but we have to go, and if we don't leave soon the removal men will be there before us,' said Dennis.

Their new home was just that, a newly built bungalow, with a much smaller garden. Although the house had everything you could wish for inside, the garden was bland paths and straight edged lawns. Soulless was Barbara's instant judgement. But there was no turning back.

They spent all the next day unpacking and moving in. Barbara was exhausted. On the following day Dennis asked Barbara to sit by the front window.

'I'm expecting a delivery and you know what these new developments are like, the driver might miss us. I'll be in the back sorting my tools, just give me a call when he arrives,' said Dennis.

It was an hour later when the lorry came slowly down the road. Barbara was lost in her book when she saw it. She rushed into the back garden to find Dennis digging a hole in the lawn.

'What are you doing, Dennis?' she said, then quietly, 'your delivery's here.'

'Good, come and give me a hand.'

Of course, Barbara didn't need to lend a hand. The friendly people from the garden centre unloaded what must have been the biggest Cherry Tree they had and trolleyed it around to the back of the bungalow. They even helped Dennis site it in the hole he'd dug.

'After all,' said Dennis after the lorry had left and they were admiring the magnificent tree, 'this is a special occasion!' They enjoyed its blossom together for many years.

One Small Step for a Journalist

EMILY HADN'T REALISED that foot fetishism was even a "thing". But her editor assured her it was and assigned her to do some research and write the story. At first, she thought it was a joke. This was her first assignment as cub reporter on the Daily Investigator and she expected to be teased, but Andy's look was serious. She started work on the assignment immediately.

The web research made her smile at first. The predilection was more common in men than women, apparently, and thinking of her boyfriend's feet she could understand why. Who would have thought that a whole Flickr album was dedicated to foot fetishism? Emily laughed aloud at some of the images.

Wiki, as ever, provided a mountain of information. It was easy to believe some of the extensive list of celebrities reputed to be turned on by feet because, Emily thought, they were all just a bit weird. But it was harder to believe of Emily's favourite heartthrob. How some of the older names came up completely bemused Emily, Elvis, really? Thomas Hardy, how could anyone know? Goethe, well Emily wasn't even sure who Goethe was, but he sounded a bit strange, so maybe.

Emily found "Well worn" ladies' high heels were commonly for sale online, the adverts always with a photo of at least one foot. They often cost more than the price of a new pair. I must remember not to send them to the charity shop, she thought.

But none of this would do for her story. It was all too easy to come by. Emily had to search deeper. She'd heard of the Dark Web but had never tried a search there. It was a tentative exploration to begin with. Emily made sure her computer was backed up and her anti-virus up to date. Then she began.

The journey that Emily took that night was dark and terrible. The personal services for sale to foot fetishists were comprehensive, but mild compared to some of the offerings she saw in the depths of the Underweb. The feet for sale, severed from corpses, came in all sizes, genders and colours, some wearing shoes, boots, slippers. One site offered feet from the exhumed bodies of famous people, but these were as widespread as pieces of the Cross in the Middle Ages.

On Emily ploughed, deep into the night, making notes and beginning to construct the article she would write. She struggled to overcome her shock at the depravity of humanity but continued to delve deeper and deeper into the pit.

Then, on a site dedicated to small feet, Emily saw it and she had to stop. She felt sick and knew she could take no more of this horror. She shut her computer down and closed the lid. She quickly wrote down what she had seen.

The short advert told an horrific story. A story all the world needed to know about.

For sale, Baby. Shoes never worn.

The Heat of the Moment

'CAREFUL INSPECTOR, IT'S all a bit messy, you'll need these.' The uniformed sergeant handed Detective Inspector Farley a pair of shoe protectors.

As he put them on Guy Farley grumbled, 'I don't want a description, just show me the body.'

Guy hadn't been surprised when he had got the call to attend a possible murder scene. Since he joined the CID fifteen years ago, he had been called to a murder every time there was a heat wave.

The body lay in the lounge of the top floor flat of the upmarket block of retirement properties. Flats here cost much more than Guy could afford, so no ordinary retirees these, but well-heeled and well spoken. New purchasers were vetted by a residents' association before they could buy to make sure they would fit in. It wasn't just money and background that were important here, but attitude and status.

The walls of the flat were decorated with photographs of the victim as a much younger woman receiving bouquets of flowers. Her picture was also prominent on the collection of old recordings, both vinyl and cd, that graced the expensively retro hi-fi set up.

The body was of a woman of about eighty. Dressed in a silk evening gown, she lay on the expensive carpet, blood from her head mingling with the Turkey Red design. An empty and blood-stained pink champagne bottle lay by her side. A quick look from a distance told Guy this was a pure murder, not a theft gone wrong. The victim still wore jewellery that would have cost Guy a year's salary.

Guy carefully padded around the flat, keeping a distance from the body. After he had done a full circuit, he returned to the sergeant.

'Have you arrested him yet?' Guy asked.

The Sergeant was perplexed, but he had known Guy ten years or so and was used to his gruff and sometimes patronising manner.

'Not yet, Guv, we're waiting for Forensics to turn up. He's bound to have left some evidence.'

'Now this, Jimmy, is exactly why I'm a DI and you're still in uniform chasing kids.'

'But the Champagne bottle, it was obviously a date, and the bottle was obviously used to batter the poor woman's brains in,' said the sergeant.

Guy shook his head slowly, as if frustrated by a small child. 'I don't doubt that the bottle was the murder weapon. But a date? I don't think so Jimmy.'

'I don't follow you guv, nothings been stolen, and she looks like she might have been entertaining, if you get my drift.'

'Look Jimmy, only one glass on the table, see? And a couple more bottles of the same champagne in the fridge, and a case under the kitchen table. It's obviously her usual tipple. Besides, look at the hi-fi, volume set to loud, huge scratch on the old recording of Carmen, and the plug yanked from the socket. I think you'll find our murderer in the flat below. And I think you'll find he hates opera.

At the Airfield

'TELL ME HONESTLY, Ben, do you love me?'

'I don't know why you're asking me that, Trisha.'

'Isn't it obvious why?'

'No, not really.'

'Well, you've never actually said those three little words.'

'What three little words?'

'Now you're teasing me. You know which words I mean.' And Trisha gave Ben a playful thump on the arm.

Ben feigned serious injury, clutching his shoulder and exclaiming loudly that she'd committed a serious assault. And he pulled that hurt face that Trisha could only ever respond to with laughter.

'But I'm serious, really I am,' said Trisha. 'We've been going out together for eighteen months now, and I don't want to live my life in limbo. You know how I feel about you, but you've never really told me.'

Trisha knew Ben wasn't the type to wear his heart on his sleeve. He liked to think things through and be certain before making decisions. That was one of the reasons she liked him so much.

'I have been thinking about us a lot lately,' he said.

'Is that why you've brought me out here. I must say, I can think of many more romantic spots than this.' Then Trisha fell silent at the implications of what she said.

If he really loved her wouldn't they be somewhere exotic, Paris, or Rome, instead of the café at this windswept airfield. Trisha's heart sank. Maybe this was it between them. A shame, she really liked Ben as a person as well as loved him. But she wasn't going to be strung along not knowing what was happening. If Ben didn't feel the same way, it was best it was over.

Yes, it would hurt, and Trisha felt her eyes begin to fill. She excused herself to regain her composure. She was not going to cry in front of Ben.

When Trisha returned Ben was standing at the window staring across the airfield towards the town on a nearby hill. She quietly stood next to him. Eventually Ben turned to her.

'Will you come outside with me? There's something I must tell you and I can't do it in here.'

'But it's the middle of February, it's freezing out there.'

'Please, Trisha, it won't take long.'

Is this it? Thought Trisha as she followed him out towards the airfield. There was a bitter breeze from the Northeast, and the temperature was near freezing. She shivered, both inwardly and outwardly, but steeled herself for whatever she was about to hear.

'Okay what do you want to say, I don't want to freeze.'

Ben was about to speak when the roar of aeroplane engines made speech impossible. He stood beside Trisha and pointed. A plane was making a low pass of the airfield trailing a banner.

"Will you marry me" it spelled out in huge letters.

Trisha turned to Ben, her head a whirl of confusion, but he pointed at a second aircraft towing another banner.

"PS I love you, Trisha" it said.

Autumn Story

It was their first home together and, like many people, Jack and Beth wanted to make it special.

'You know,' said Beth, 'things are going to have to change when Autumn comes.'

'I know, I know. There's a lot to do but I'm up to it,' said Jack.

'Well, it won't be long now, so I hope you are,' said Beth.

Jack was true to his word. Despite working all the overtime he could get, the young couple needed every penny, he still found time to tidy the garden and dig out the brambles and nettles that had taken root during the summer.

After spending a rare spare Saturday making sure all the fences were fixed and the paving was straight and level Jack paused for a few minutes. He went to the fridge to get himself a beer as a reward for a job well done only to find it was the last one.

That evening, as they relaxed, Jack said, 'there's no beer left. I'll pick some up tomorrow.'

'Are you sure we can afford it?' said Beth, 'Autumn will be here soon with all the extra expense. We don't really know how much money we'll need.'

'You're right, I can do without for a few months, until we see how we are.'

When the weather was fine, and he wasn't at work, Jack would continue working in the garden. When the weather was wet, he would work in the house, decorating and laying new carpet. Occasionally the couple would make a trip to the shops and buy something together, but not very often.

'It won't be long now,' said Beth one day, 'I think Autumn is just around the corner.'

Jack worked harder, did even more overtime. He was lucky, he enjoyed his work. He didn't enjoy it as much as being at home with Beth, but they both knew it was the best for Jack to be earning as much as he could just now.

Then one Wednesday afternoon while he was at work Jack got a text from Beth. He told his boss he had to leave; Beth was in hospital.

He drove as quickly as he dared but the roads were narrow and twisty, and it seemed like the day that every harvest tractor in the land was on the road. Eventually he made it to the hospital and found somewhere to park.

Jack ran into reception and asked the way to Beth's ward. The volunteer receptionist told him, but also told him not to run. He had never walked so fast in all his life. Finally, he was at Beth's bedside, she seemed to be sleeping, he didn't know if he should wake her when she turned, opened her eyes and smiled at him.

'What do think of Autumn, then?' said Beth.

Jack reached down, a tear in his eye. 'She's beautiful,' he said, bewitched by the daughter he cradled in his arms.

Short Term Placement

I WOULD NEVER have thought about fostering if a friend hadn't suggested it. Although I have lots of nieces and nephews, I've never had children of my own so I didn't think they would take me seriously as a possible foster parent. But they did. The first children I looked after were straight forward and just needed a quiet, safe place for a while. Just until their families got organised.

Gradually the agency began to send me children who were a more challenging, and I seemed to do a good job because they all seemed happy. Then they sent me Steven.

Steven was six and the social worker said he could be "difficult". I soon realised what an understatement that was.

He demolished the rockery I had built the previous summer in a single morning. The wildlife pond became a target for pots and garden tools. At least I knew where I could find my trowel.

I tried to show him what it was like, to grow things and enjoy them. He pulled up the petunias and trampled the lettuce.

That year was horrendous. I worried I might fail him and have to send him back, back into care. What would become of him then? Crime, drugs, who knows? I gritted my teeth and hung on.

It was the strawberries that began the change. Instead of destroying them he ate them. Not one passed my lips that summer. But I saw him smile for the first time. A red mouthed, full of strawberry smile. I laughed out loud, my first laugh since Steven arrived.

'Wait until you taste the raspberries,' I said. He tasted them. He liked them. I didn't get a single one that year.

Steven began following me around the garden. He started asking questions. He began to learn the seasons, the way of sowing and harvesting. He slowly learnt to wait and to share.

He started to understand what the garden needed, how to care for it, how to grow his own plants. I watched him delight in their abundance.

I was utterly unprepared for the reappearance of his birth mother, demanding to have him back. He'd been with me for seven years. The longest "short term placement" I ever had. I thought he would stay forever. I loved him, as if I were his mother.

Steven looked at me, wise beyond his years. 'You've taught me so much but now I have to go and make my own garden. Don't worry, I will come back.'

I was bereft, lost. When the agency contacted me I couldn't accept another child. I felt awful, guilty.

Three months went by until the day he kept his word and returned.

'I've come for some cuttings,' he said.

'Who's that with you?' I said.

'This is Peter, my brother, he's seven.' We watched as Peter began to kick over the chrysanthemums.

Then Steven said, 'I think he needs to learn about gardening, will you teach him?'

Celebrating

She was late.

He could tell, as soon as she came in, before he even saw her. The lengthy pause between the opening and then crashing of the front door, the shoes kicked off rather than gently prised from her feet. And, of course, the singing.

He knew she couldn't sing; she knew she couldn't sing, and the only time she sang was after she'd been to the pub. Tom had lost count of how many times he'd had the conversation with her, she had to stop, they couldn't afford it, he couldn't stand it. No matter what he said it all came back to this. She tried; she really did try. For maybe a week, ten days, it would be the old Rosie back again, but then she would fail again, and Tom was at his wits end.

He was standing with arms folded when she

came into the kitchen. 'You've been drinking again,' he said.

'I've only had a couple, I'm not drunk,' said Rosie.

Tom could see she had been in worse states, but she certainly would be unfit to drive, and he was relieved she took the bus to work.

'You've still been drinking, after all we agreed.'

'I know Tom, but I was just…'

'Don't even bother trying to explain. I don't want to hear any more excuses. I've heard them all before.'

'But Tom, really…'

'Don't say anymore, it won't make any difference. We've already decided that this would be the last time for us.'

'I was celebrating, that's all.'

'Celebrating! Again. What was it this time? The cat's birthday, the anniversary of you first being sacked. You're always celebrating and now the excuses have worn too thin.'

'No, really, Tom this time it was a celebration.'

'I hope you've been celebrating being single again because I've had enough. You knew what would happen as soon as you stepped in the pub door. While you've been boozing, I've been packing.'

'Tom, don't go, really don't, life will be different now.'

'You make these promises all the time when you're drunk and then never keep them. I can't cope anymore. It's time I thought about myself instead of you.'

Tom took the stairs two at a time when he went to fetch his suitcase. He was angry and needed to use some energy. How could she do this again. She knew what it did to him.

He came downstairs and began putting on his coat.

'You shouldn't go, Tom, you really shouldn't,' said Rosie.

'I'll call for the rest of my stuff in a few days, when you're sober.'

'But Tom I was only celebrating…'

'Just stop, don't speak to me anymore, I've had enough of your lies and deception. I'm leaving.' Tom slammed the front door behind him.

'… winning thirty million on the lottery,' said Rosie to the closed door. 'I guess now I'll have to spend it all by myself.' And she smiled.

Dinner Date

When Mike told me he had something special to show me I thought it might be his usual sort of thing, a novelty mug, or an annoying, squeaky, toy. These were the level of gifts we usually exchanged. But this is different. The thrill I feel is tinged with apprehension as I pause before pulling the bag open. What could this be, and why would Mike be giving it to me?

Mike and I have shared the same office for seventeen years, and in that time we have got to know each other well. Working in Customer services can be difficult sometimes, and sharing the difficulties of work has gradually grown to sharing the difficulties of life. Mike knows my husband died in Afghanistan, and I know Mike's wife left him. We occasionally share a drink after work, but our relationship is purely a working one. Mike used to ask me out sometimes, but although good company he isn't my type, so I've always declined. Until today. Today, Mike said, is a special occasion and he wanted to say something to me, and would I have dinner with him.

Now I am sitting opposite this man I have known longer than anybody outside my family and he gives me this small black bag bearing the crest of an expensive jeweller.

'Please open it' says Mike, 'and tell me what you think.'

'Oh, Mike, I'm not sure I can…'

'Just have a look, you have such good taste, tell me if you like it.'

As I open the bag, I hear Mike talking, but everything becomes muffled and I'm not sure what he's saying. I pull out a small, black velvet box with the same crest. I feel my eyes begin to fill. I spring the box open and there is a solitaire engagement ring, the sister of the one I am wearing. I don't know what to think. A part of me is flattered, but a part of me thinks "how thoughtless, to offer something so close to the memory of my husband". Now my vision is blurred as well as my hearing, and I let out a sob.

Through the fog that surrounds me I hear Mike's voice.

'Is it really that bad?' he says.

'No, Mike, it's beautiful, but I.…'

I am thinking of the grand romantic gesture that preceded my husband's proposal. The chase halfway across the continent, the bended knee and moonlight on the Aegean shore. And here I am, in this second-rate restaurant with this man who just doesn't have, you know, it.

'Mike I'm really sorry but I don't think I…'

'You don't think she'll like it do you? I can take it back tomorrow; she hasn't seen it yet. Will you help me choose another one?'

I'm confused. 'She?' I ask.

'Yes, like I've been saying, Jill in accounts, but if she won't like it, I can get another.'

Emergency Call-Out

'THANK GOODNESS YOUR here, we're very grateful.'

'When I got your urgent message, I knew I just had to get here as fast as I could.'

'Do you need anything? A drink, something to eat.'

'It was a long journey, but maybe that should wait. Perhaps you'd best show me the animal and I'll see what I can do.'

'He's upstairs in Jenny's room.'

Mrs Salinger led me to one of the bedrooms. As she opened the door I could hear the sobs of a young girl.

'Jenny, I've brought someone to look at him for you.'

Jenny was crouched on the floor with her arms around the animal's neck. Her tear-stained face turned towards us. She didn't speak, but I could tell she was trying to control her tears.

'Don't worry honey, I've seen lots like him before,' I said.

'Will you really be able to help him mister…'

'Just call me Tod, there's no need, nor time, for formalities in a situation such as this,' I said.

'Thank you mister… Tod, but can you help him?'

'I'll need to take a closer look before I can be sure. Would it be all right if I just get down on the ground with you and check him out? It might help keep him calm if you were to stroke him while I had a look, could you do that for me?'

Jenny nodded, and I knelt and examined the beast. A fine example it was too, and I was confident I could help.

'I'm fairly sure I can help the old fella, but I've got to ask a big favour of Jenny here, Mrs Salinger. Do you think she could leave me alone with him for about an hour?'

'Jenny, can you do that for Tod, so he can do his healing work?'

Jenny took a deep breath and then nodded.

'And maybe when I've done there'll be time for a drink and something to eat Mrs Salinger?'

'Certainly, Tod, there'll be a fine meal for you when you've finished your work here.'

I ushered the two out of the room, opened my bag and got to work. As I worked the smell of cooking wafted up and made my stomach growl. The animal didn't respond, but that didn't surprise me.

It was fifty minutes later when I opened the door and called out, 'Jenny, come on up, I'm done now.'

We passed each other on the stairs, me heading for a well-earned meal, Jenny rushing to be reunited with the love of her life.

'Was it a terrible problem?' said Mrs Salinger while I'm in the kitchen eating my supper.

'Just listen,' I said, 'no squeaking or grinding. It just needed a couple of new bearings and a drop of oil.'

'I don't know how to thank you,' said Mrs Salinger, 'Jenny was bereft.'

'No thanks are necessary, Mrs Salinger. It's all part of a day's work for a Rocking Horse Whisperer.'

Water Bottles

This story was written during the pandemic when social distancing was required.

I was out for a run, my daily exercise, and I'd stopped to sit on a park bench for a couple of minutes to get my breath. That's when I first saw him. I pulled an earpiece out. 'Sorry, what did you say?'

'I asked if I could sit here,' he said.

'Sure, it's more than two metres away.' I was putting the earpiece back in when he said, 'It's just that I need to sit down for a minute.'

That's when I took a proper look at him. He was an old guy, maybe about a hundred, I don't know, but ancient, wrinkly and grey. He was wearing a grubby old coat and he had a stick he was leaning on. He tried to lower himself onto the bench but his knees sort of gave way halfway down and he landed with a thump. It knocked my water bottle over.

'I'm sorry, really I didn't mean to…'

'Hey, it's alright, nothing broken, nothing spilled, got the lid on see.' I showed him the bottle.

'What's that? A vacuum flask?' he said.

I laughed. 'Haven't you seen a water bottle before?'

'Not that colour,' he said, 'and we used to call them canteens.'

'What's wrong with the colour?'

'It's a bit bright,' he said.

'That means I don't lose it in the grass. I can see it miles away.'

I unscrewed the lid and took a drink. 'No plastic, see, not like the old bottles. I'm doing my bit.'

'Doing your bit?'

'Yeah, for the environment, not using plastic, saving the planet.'

'Good, it needs saving.'

'I can't offer you a drink, social distancing and all that.'

'I've got my own,' he said. He rummaged in the inside pocket of his old, tattered coat and pulled out this ancient thing.

It was a sort of bottle, but it was wrapped up in some old, brownish cloth, and had frayed straps around it. Tatty it was, with holes in the cloth. I could see the dull metal underneath. Wouldn't want to drink out of it myself.

I watched as the old man pulled a cork out of the top. A cork! Then he took a drink. 'It's always best to use your own canteen,' he said.

I laughed. 'It sure is,' I said and took another swig of water, then watched as he took a swig from his bottle.

'You don't want to leave that anywhere,' I said, 'you'll never find it again, that colour.'

'That was the idea when I got it, that it's hard to spot.'

'Why wouldn't you want to find it?'

'Not me, hard for others to see,' he said.

'It looks ancient. Where'd 'you get it?'

'I got it when I was doing my bit,' he said. 'But back then we were only saving the country, not the planet.'

Lads and Dads Week

IT SOUNDED LIKE a good idea. A week away with my two sons, ten and twelve, all blokes together, give Abigail a break. It would also drag the two of them away from the obsession that's occupied most of their summer and driven me and her crazy. We pack tents and stoves and sleeping bags into the car and set off on the five-hour drive to the 'Lads and Dads Week' campsite.

It doesn't matter how much stuff they've got to occupy them in the back, it's not enough. Soon they're bickering with each other. I thought my daily commute was stressful, but with two boys in the back of a packed car on a sweltering summer day, stressful isn't the word.

When they start chanting in unison, "Are we there yet, are we there yet," I lose it. I yell at them, but they take no notice and carry on. Usually I'm good at joining in these games, but the A303 is choc-a-bloc with traffic, my back aches and there's nowhere to stop for miles.

I know I shouldn't have, but what parent hasn't? Turned around when they're driving and yelled at them in the back. Who hasn't done that? And most of the time it's okay, isn't it?

It would have been okay this time, but I turned the wheel and we hit the kerb. We weren't going fast. Only about walking pace. There must have been a weakness in the tyre, or a sharp stone, but something caused the puncture. It wasn't serious, there were no injuries, but I felt the tyre deflate, and my mood followed. I put on the emergency flashers and pulled in as far as possible. A Saturday in August on the A303 and I'm causing a major traffic jam.

I get out and hustle the kids out of the car and behind the crash barriers. The traffic might only be doing five mph, but they are boys aren't they, so better off behind the barrier.

I need to get the spare on, but I can't manage with the emergency jack, not with this traffic. If another car nudged us when I was taking the wheel off it could be nasty. I phone the AA, explain where I am.

They arrive surprisingly quickly, from the opposite direction, and do a U-turn in the road. The traffic stops to let them. I feel the withering contempt of other drivers for causing a delay.

As the AA man gets his tool kit out, I begin unloading our stuff from the boot. I push most of it into the back seat where the boys have been sitting. The boys are quiet now. I think they realise how serious this is.

The AA man comes around just as I lift the floor of the boot to get at the spare wheel. He sees it at the same time as I do. Where the spare wheel is supposed to be, there are two skateboards.

Proof of Identity

It's all very well you saying you're his lordship's son, but how am I supposed to know that? If I go and let you in and you turn out to be some sort of imposter, then there'll be the devil to pay when he gets back. Likely as not I'll lose my job. And maybe even much more than my job. No, no, it's more than my life's worth to let you in without his lordship's express allowing, you know, him himself saying so.

I know you're wearing his lordship's colours, but that doesn't mean anything, you might have stolen them from some poor soul's dead body after the battle. I heard the fearsomeness of it all the way up here. Thousands of dead, I should imagine. Took all the other men from this here castle did his lordship. So you see, just wearing his lordship's colours doesn't prove you're one of his lordship's men. Were I to let you in you might just take it upon yourself to slit my gizzard and then where would I be?

It doesn't help you losing your temper and talking to me like that you know. And there's no need to talk about my mother like that either. I mean really, what a thing to say about my sainted old mum. Not to mention what you said about my father, although he was a bit of a bas… well anyway, talking like that won't get you anywhere, I've got my orders and I'm sticking to them. And if you can't be civil to a poor guardsman who's been on duty all-night then I won't talk to you at all.

Well, as you've put it so politely, I'll listen to your request again. Mind your language though. I'll not have my relatives besmirched in that way. I mean, how would you like it if I said that about your parentage? You'd have my head off as soon as look at me, but that's the gentry for you, isn't it? A law unto themselves they are, but where's the justice for us poor serfs and such? No, for us it's touch my cap and "yes milord, no milord, three bags full milord" and God help any of us that complains, begging the almighty's forgiveness for taking his name in vain of course. So, what was it you were saying again?

It's like I say, despite you being all polite, I just don't really know who you are do I? It's all very well you giving me the word of a gentleman, and I don't doubt you are one, that you'll not harm me. But supposing I let you in, and you start ransacking his lordship's treasure house, all looting and pillaging like, and then his lordship turns up and here I am, all right as nine pence looking on. He'll think I was in cahoots with you, and it'd be off with my bleeding head as soon as you can say jack sparrow, wouldn't it?

It might be urgent for you, but quite frankly, I just don't see the urgency myself. What's wrong with waiting until his lordship gets back from the battle? He's sure to have won, and then he'll be really generous, and you'll be let in and be able to enjoy the victory celebrations and I'll get a gold coin for being especially effective at my duty and not letting you in afore he got here.

What's that, you telling me, his lordship's not coming back, he's been killed in the battle? Get away with you, that would never happen to his lordship. He's a famous fighter, he'd never get himself killed on the field. Well yes now you come to mention it, that does look a bit like his lordship's horse, but he might have fallen off it and you might have stolen it.

Yes, I do recognise his lordship's ruby ring which what he always wore every day, and never took off in his whole life. And the severed hand that's still wearing it, it's definitely his lordship's. Oh dear me, the poor fellows had his hand cut off by thieving vagabonds after his jewels, what is the world coming to.

What's that, can you speak up a bit, I can hardly hear you over the galloping sound of thousands of horsemen in the distance? Oh yes, I do know that hat, that is his lordship's, and I recognise the head that's still wearing it. Woe, a thousand woes, my poor Lord has been murdered in battle. What? Yes, I've got to admit it does bear a certain familial likeness to your good self. I do declare you are his lordship's son. I am most regretfully sorry your lordship, please forgive a poor guardsman for doing his duty.

Hang on, there's no need to shout and scream, I'll be down right away to let you in, as soon as I can get my creaking knees down the hundred and eighty-seven steps from this tower. Shouldn't take no more than five minutes. You see, being on my own, I can't work the windlass to lift the main gate and drop the drawbridge. If you can just hang on and be patient a bit. Mind you I should hide from that bunch of fighting men if I were you, they look like they mean business.

You're welcome captain. I didn't mind delaying the bugger at all. Him and his father were a pair of ruthless rogues that terrorised the poor peasants about these parts. Now I'm hoping I can remind you about our agreement. You know, the one about me getting a reward for helping you out with his lordship's son and heir and letting you into the castle. Here can you tell your soldiers to get their hands off me. What was that you were telling your men, did I mis-hear? It sounded like "hang the treacherous malingerer."

Lunch for Two

It needed repairs and redecorating everywhere. It cost all the money Mark and Laura could raise, but they loved the old house they bought and were looking forward to moving to the small town.

The couple had a precious two weeks off work to clean and decorate their new home and furnish it with the few pieces of cheap furniture their credit cards allowed.

On the first day they met Matilda, their neighbour. Although they were busy, they knew how important good neighbours were. They happily chatted with Matilda for half an hour every day as she passed on her way into town.

At the end of the fortnight, they looked at their bank account.

'I wanted to take you to dinner, with champagne,' said Mark, 'but it might just be beer and a cheese sandwich.'

'Let's try the restaurant in town,' said Laura, 'lunch shouldn't be expensive.'

They gathered together all the money they could find, about twenty pounds, and set off hoping it would be enough.

Mark said he would like the Sirloin steak with all the trimmings, and Laura said she would enjoy the Roasted Mediterranean vegetables with sweet potato fries. But they couldn't afford those.

'Are you ready to order?'

'Can we have two cheese salads please,' said Mark.

'We're trying out some new starters and the chef wants feedback. Would you be willing to try them for free?' said the waiter.

Mark didn't hesitate. Or ask what they were.

Mark had Scallops with chorizo and hazelnut picada, while Laura had Triple cheese and tarragon stuffed mushrooms. They lingered over these delicious dishes. When their main courses were delivered, they weren't the cheese salads they'd ordered, but the steak and Mediterranean vegetables they had wished for.

Mark began to object, 'I'm sorry, this isn't what we ordered.'

'I must have misheard,' said the waiter, sweeping away.

'What shall we do?' said Mark.

'Let's just enjoy it,' said Laura tucking in.

When their empty plates were cleared away, they were replaced by exotic desserts.

'We didn't order these,' said Mark, beginning to panic.

'I'm sorry, I can't take them back to the kitchen, have them anyway,' said the waiter.

'We'll be washing up here for a week,' said Laura when they had finished. 'Look the sign says pay at the till.'

Mark reached into his pocket for the few grubby pounds he had as they approached the till and the restaurant's owner.

'Someone has already paid,' said the proprietor.

Mark and Laura looked at each other with disbelief.

'And they left this for you.' And he pulled a bottle bag from behind the counter.

It was an expensive bottle of champagne, the label around its neck said, "Welcome to your new home".

That evening the proprietor phoned Matilda. 'Yes, they were just as lovely as you said they were, and you should have seen the ear to ear smiles they wore as they left. You can pay me next week. And Matilda, the champagne's on me.'

Man at Work

'THIS WON'T TAKE long, ten minutes maybe,' said Tony sounding supremely confident.

Christabel knew him well and to her it didn't look like a ten-minute job. 'Are you sure?' she said.

'Really,' said Tony, 'these things aren't that hard. I've done similar stuff before. Maybe twenty minutes at most. Leave it to me.'

Christabel left it to him. She thought he'd be at least half an hour. She spent thirty minutes in the greenhouse before putting the kettle on.

'I've made you coffee,' she said, looking at the growing chaos in the spare room.

'Fantastic, just what I need. I haven't finished yet, it's just that it's a bit more…'

'Complicated than you first thought?' said Christabel.

'Yes, just a bit, but I think I've got the hang of it

now. I should be done in another half hour,' said Tony.

Christabel looked around the room, doubting half an hour would be enough. 'It will be time for lunch in an hour and afterwards…'

'I'll be finished by lunchtime, definitely.'

Christabel heard frustration mixed in with Tony's usual confidence. She went back to her garden.

An hour later Christabel was again in the kitchen and prepared a quick, snack lunch for them both. She called up the stairs. 'Lunch is ready, Tony. Are you coming or am I eating alone?'

'I'm coming, I'll just… oh...'

Christabel couldn't make out the last word Tony said but was fairly sure it would be unrepeatable.

'Do you want me to give you a hand?' said Christabel, after they finished lunch.

'No, no, I'll be fine. It's nearly done. Besides, you're going out, aren't you?'

'It's only coffee with friends, if you need me to help, I'll cancel.'

'You go out, I'll be finished before you're back.

Christabel met her friends, did some shopping, and came home. Tony still wasn't finished.

'It's taken nearly all day,' said Christabel handing Tony a mug of tea.

'Yes, but it's nearly there isn't it. You can see there's not much more to do.'

Christabel said nothing and went to prepare dinner.

They hardly spoke during dinner. Christabel had asked how it was going but Tony's response closed that conversation. After they'd finished Christabel said, 'I'll clear up, you go and get the blooming thing finished.'

Tony scurried back upstairs.

At eight pm she felt sorry for him and took him a cup of tea. 'I'm going to watch Poldark and have a glass of wine, why don't you leave it until tomorrow?'

'I said I'll do it today and I will,' said Tony. He didn't sound happy.

The final credits were running, and Christabel was wondering if she should have a second glass of the Malbec when Tony finally staggered downstairs and slumped into an armchair. He poured himself a generous glass.

'Finished then?' said Christabel.

'Yes,' said Tony, quaffing.

'Maybe we shouldn't…'

'Don't say it, just don't say it,' said Tony.

But Christabel said it anyway. 'Maybe we shouldn't have gone self-assembly.'

The Gift

SHE TELLS ME it is an unusual gift, as she hands me the small, tightly wrapped, package.

'But what can it be,' I muse, turning the package over in my hands, feeling the weight, the shape.

'Open it!' calls one of the guests, soon joined by a chorus from the rest of the party gathered to celebrate my birthday.

It is late. This is the last of the gifts. A table behind me is crammed with boxes and packages of all different shapes and sizes. From the tiny packet containing the diamond solitaire cufflinks from my latest lover to the life size photograph of the new Porsche parked outside, a gift from one of my most favoured business associates.

Although it is late, I do not want the party to end so I delay. I signal the staff and glasses are again filled with Cristal champagne.

I turn through the circle of people gathered round me; glass held high. 'First we must toast the gift and the giver,' I announce. Everyone cheers, but do I hear a certain weariness in the cheer? Are some people less than enthusiastic at my celebration? My steely gaze wanders over them, but every face I see is happy and smiling. Then it occurs to me that I don't actually recognise the giver of this last gift. I turn full circle to look at her. There is something about her that is familiar, but I cannot recall a name. It is very late, I think, and I have had a bit to drink, and there are a lot of people here.

'So' I say, 'A toast to… er,' and look quizzically at her, expecting her to fill in the name missing from my memory. But she does not. She returns my gaze coolly and waits.

'I'm sorry, dearie, But I seem to have forgotten your name,' I say.

She does not reply but holds my gaze with a frankness few can manage when I look them in the eye. I falter, my usual confidence falling away into doubt. I gather myself. This is not how people behave towards me. They are deferential, they respond to my wishes, they understand my great wealth, and they understand that with great wealth comes great power.

'Come on dearie,' I say. 'Remind me of your name.' I am beginning to lose my patience with this person, despite her having the sort of drop-dead gorgeous looks that would normally have me buying her all sorts of goodies. And expecting payment in kind of course.

She looks at me coolly. There is something I find attractive in the confidence with which she holds herself. Relaxed, poised and with complete self-assurance. I take a sip from my glass and notice she doesn't have one.

'Are you not toasting my birthday... er ... look tell me your name will you, it will make our conversation much more pleasant.' I call the waiter to bring a glass for her, but she waves him away with an almost imperceptible movement. A gesture so subtle that few would have noticed it. Now I am curious.

'OK so you don't want a glass of champagne, that's fine, but allow me to express my great gratitude for your generous gift,' I say, taking a step towards her, as if to take her arm.

There is something in the small movement of her hand that stops me from moving closer to her, or reaching out to touch her, something I cannot fathom, but I begin to have a sense of foreboding.

Finally, she speaks.

'You do not know me, and my name is unimportant. As for the gift, it is merely a mirror of your own generosity. I trust it will bring you all that you deserve. But first, you must open it.'

My attention turns to the small parcel. I hear those gathered around me encouraging me to open it, their voices sound tinged with boredom. As I begin to pick at the packaging, I think about the people here and realise that I cannot call them friends, they are but toadies and lackeys who only desire to benefit from my wealth.

I turn to the mystery woman, but she is gone.

I open the parcel. It is empty. A groan comes from the crowd, and I am suddenly angry. I shout at them and tell them to leave. Shortly I am alone. It is then that I notice that there is a picture on the inside of the wrapper. It is a photograph of two tramps sitting on a park bench. They are skinny with matted hair and gappy teeth. Their clothes are shabby and dirty. They are people who I would routinely ignore. But there is something about the picture that is incongruous to me. I look again. They are both smiling at each other. There is a sense of contentment in the picture. The tramps look happy! I look at it for a moment then toss it aside.

I press the button that will summon the staff to clear the mess left by the celebration and retreat to my bedroom suite.

As I prepare to retire, I stand for a while gazing out over the metropolis stretched out before me. The penthouse I own represents the proceeds of a particularly lucrative set of deals during the dot-com boom years before the turn of the century. That and the timely withdrawal from the market before it all fell apart is the basis of the huge wealth I have since accumulated. A giant conglomerate of companies and trusts with fingers in most of the financial institutions of the world. Nothing as risky as tech companies for me now. But finance is a different thing. Everybody needs to borrow money, and it's so respectable.

I retire to bed and sleep late, which is unfortunate.

The next day is Monday 8th October 2008, Black Monday.

When I finally wake, I have hundreds of messages on my phone and computer. All demanding attention. Huge margin calls are being made on leveraged market positions I hold, in sums my staff are not authorised to deal with. So there has been a delay in settling and exiting these positions. Too long a delay. The cheap lines of credit I have negotiated to be able to take the best advantage of a rising market have now exposed me to huge losses. I start to try to contact people. Even for me it is too slow. The phone lines, the internet, the mobile systems, they are all being overloaded by people trying to do what I am trying to do and cover their losses. But it is too late. By the end of the day, I owe several times more than the assets I have, a considerable sum.

I contact some of my business associates but unusually none of them are available to speak to me. I leave messages but none get back to me. I call my staff in to tell them I won't be able to pay their wages this month, and perhaps not for a very long time. They appear to be quite sanguine about it. One of the maids suggests she makes some tea, and I thank her and agree. Other members of the staff also suggest doing small tasks to make my life a little more comfortable. Although none of these things in themselves will make an ounce of difference in the bigger picture I am impressed by their kindly thoughts and humanity. I know I have been a hard taskmaster, but I have paid them well in the past. They must have appreciated the money. I think about the staff a little while I wait for the tea to arrive and realise I don't really know anything about the maid who offered to make it, nor really any of the staff. These people who are offering me succour have meant nothing to me before today. I begin to wish I had taken a little more time to get to know them rather than delivering orders.

After an hour or so I begin to wonder where the tea is. I ring the bell. No one responds. I go and look for the staff. They have all left and taken anything of value that they could.

Over the next few weeks all my bank accounts are emptied, my credit cards refused, and creditors are persistently trying to collect what I owe, which of course I cannot pay. The paintings are taken from the walls, likewise the antique furniture. The Porsche, its fuel tank practically empty, is towed away. When I cannot pay the phone company I am cut off. My mobile has long since gone, and now the power company say they will cut off all power to the penthouse next week.

The weather is cold, and winter is coming. I put on my warmest clothes, pack a bag with what personal possessions I can carry and take my private lift to the ground floor. In the lobby the janitor at the security desk greets me in an almost friendly manner, when he sees me with a bag packed.

'Going on holiday, are we sir?' he says.

'You could say that,' I reply. 'And I don't think I'll be needing these again,' I say as I lay the keys to the penthouse on the counter.

I can't remember where I slept that first night, only that I was cold and frightened. Gradually, as months and years passed, I learn a different lifestyle. I learn where a warm bed could be had for the night. I learn where free soup could be had in exchange for singing a hymn or two, regardless of your beliefs. I learn where you can have an aching tooth extracted free of charge. I learn where you can swap your threadbare coat for one which is not quite so threadbare. I learn that when you have nothing, you also have nothing to lose.

One day I am sitting on a park bench enjoying the sunshine with my friend Tommy, another "gentleman of the road", when along comes this lass, must be a journalist, and offers me £5 to take my photograph.

I whistle through the gap in my teeth. 'Five pounds eh, but what about my mate Tommy?' I say.

'That's up to you,' she says.

I turn to Tommy and say with a smile 'Well that's two pounds fifty each then.' He smiles back at me, and I hear the camera click.

A Day at the Beach

I IMAGINED US sitting on the beach, watching the sun go down, the most romantic moment of our day out together. Just me and Lucy, alone. What could go wrong?

I was surprised she'd agreed to come with me to the coast, but she said she loved the sea, and it was a hot, fine day. When I pulled up outside her house, she had two enormous beach bags with her. All essential stuff she reassured me.

I thought of us splashing about in the sea for an hour and then stretching out, in our bathing suits, together, on a blanket, somewhere quiet. I hoped she'd have a bikini. She did. She had it on under the t-shirt and denim shorts she wore. She looked fabulous. 'Come on, let's get in the water,' I said.

'Just a minute,' she said.

And she pulled a wet suit from one of her bags

and put it on. Then snorkelling equipment and flippers came from the other bag.

There weren't many people on the beach, but safety flags flew and there was a lifeguard in distinctive red trunks atop a tall chair.

Lucy waved at him as we passed. He smiled and waved back.

'I love being in the sea,' she said as she rinsed her mask with salty water.

After half an hour I was bored of watching her as she paddled, head under water, up and down. She was a much better swimmer than I.

I swam ashore to sit on the blanket and watch. I went and had an Ice cream, I bought and read a newspaper. After three long hours I saw her stand up, take off her flippers and wade out of the water.

Halfway back she stopped by the lifeguard's chair. I saw her speak. He laughed and climbed down to talk to her. I watched them in animated conversation, laughing and joking with each other. What did she think she was doing? She came here with me. Then I saw them hug. She put her arms around him and squeezed herself into him. I was livid. How could she do this in full view. When they finally broke apart, she gave him a quick kiss, smiled, then continued up the beach.

Now I was furious as well as bored. How dare she flirt with another man while she's out with me.

'What's the matter,' she said when she got back,

'you look cross.'

I looked at her coldly as she dried her hair. 'I'm leaving now. You haven't time for that.'

'I thought we had all day.'

'We had, but after that, I'm leaving now.'

'After what?'

'Don't give me that, you know what, flirting with lover boy down there.'

'You mean Liam? He's...'

'Liam is it. Liam and Lucy, you'll make a lovely couple, maybe you should go back with him.'

She picked up her bags and threw her wetsuit over an arm.

'Alright, I will. After all, he is my brother.'

Rhubarb Rhubarb

We have so much in common. We like the same music, movies, everything. But mostly we both love food. Eating is our great pleasure. We have adventurous tastes. Thai, Japanese, Turkish, Mongolian, we try them all.

I ask her to marry me one Sunday morning. She is at my flat and there is nothing for breakfast but bread fit only for toast and that thing that divides the nation. A jar of Marmite.

'But I love Marmite,' she says.

We look for, and find, a place together. It's a tiny house, but we can afford it.

There's a small garden and we chat to our neighbour, an old bloke living alone. He says he's dividing his rhubarb roots. Would we like some? Rhubarb, the other food that divides the nation. I feel a trembling in the space that loves her. We look at each other and I give a tiny nod just as she does.

'We love rhubarb,' she says. I agree.

'Don't pull any this year or it won't thrive', advises our neighbour.

A fortnight later the old man has a fall. He's moved to a care home and the house is put up for sale. It sells quickly and a young couple move in. We see them in the garden digging up the rhubarb and bagging it for the bin men. They let us know their negative view of the plant in a way that includes most of our favourite foods. They have no taste for the exotic and high praise for local fast-food outlets. We nod politely and glance longingly at our small, unproductive, rhubarb patch.

That spring the rhubarb pokes above the ground, but we heed our old neighbour's advice and don't pull any. It feels a travesty to buy rhubarb when we have our own growing, so we go the whole year without.

The following March the bright red points of our rhubarb come again. One Saturday, we pull the first three sticks.

We play a game we have often played.

'Stewed or crumble?' she asks.

'Stewed of course,' I reply, she nods.

'Custard or cream?' I ask.

'Always custard,' she replies, and I agree.

'I can't believe you've done that' she says, anger

in her voice, as I place the bowl of rhubarb and custard before her.

'Done what?' I ask.

'You've put the rhubarb in first, and the custard on top. It's ridiculous, what did you do that for?'

'I always have my rhubarb like that, what's wrong with it?'

'It's just so wrong. How could you.'

And we have a frightful argument. Crockery and rhubarb all over the kitchen. It's our first real fight. She insists it's custard first and I insist it's rhubarb first. We make up eventually. But for fifty-eight years, whenever we eat rhubarb and custard, she has it her way and I have it mine. It just goes to show, opposites do attract.

Rock Climbing

THE RAIN DID not make the climb easier. But he was halfway up the crag when it began and had to keep going, it would be riskier to climb down than to continue to the top.

It hadn't been too difficult so far, but here he was at the hardest part. It was dangerous too; he'd known one climber who had fallen here and heard of many others. He wondered if he'd made a mistake, deciding to freeclimb here. Balancing with legs splayed on steady footholds and his left hand with a solid grip at shoulder height he peered up at the rockface. The rain fell vertically, drops landing on his eyes as he looked at his right hand stretching up to the handhold. It was a long stretch, at the limit of his reach, and the hold wasn't large, he got three fingers on and found no room for a fourth.

Just above was a larger hold. He could reach that if he pushed himself off with his left foot. But if his fingers missed it, or it crumbled, didn't hold, he would tumble, fall, eighty-five feet, a killing fall. He lived by the Law of the Rock; three points of contact at all times. He'd known some who had been careless of this law and paid the price.

His fingers complained as he tested the hold, pulling down to ensure it was firm. It held, it would hold, he was sure of that, surer than he was of his fingers as he began to transfer his weight upward through shoulder, arm, wrist, hand into those three fingers clutching the tiny ledge of rock. With his fingers locked in place he began to ease his weight from his left foot.

His fingers screamed their distress as his left foot, now free of the rock, scrabbled for the hold he knew was there, but could not see. A small stone, dislodged, clattered down the rockface, his foot slipped on lichen. His fingers redoubled their agonised clamour. He tried again, a little higher, a little more to the left. There! His foot found the hold, but, ignoring the increasing demands from his right hand, he again went through the ritual; test, try, transfer. And as his foot began to bear some of his weight his fingers quietened their complaints.

Now his right foot searched for its next hold and finding it, was followed by his left hand. At last he could release his right hand from its cramped hold and seek the next. The climb became easier. On and up, one limb at a time; try, test, transfer. Finally, he rolled onto the summit gasping for breath, quietening his pounding heart, slowing the adrenaline rushing through his blood, grinning irrepressibly.

There was a friendly smile and a mug of tea waiting for him.

'I really don't understand this at all,' said Michelle, 'you could have just walked up the path with me.'

David knew, then, that Michelle was definitely not "the one".

Julie's Room

It is a year since our beautiful daughter was killed. Julie was nineteen years old and beginning her second year at university when she met her murderer. All we know is that her mutilated body was found in a canal, and the police were unable to find either motive or killer.

It is late and raining when the knock on our door disturbs us. When I open it, there stands a girl, maybe twelve or thirteen. She's wearing a school uniform I don't recognise with a bag hanging off one shoulder. She is dripping wet.

'Please can I come in?' she says, 'I'm so cold.'

By now Linda has arrived at the door. Her maternal instincts, supressed for the last year, kick in immediately, and before I can speak she's welcoming the stray into the warmth of our kitchen. How she comes to be at our door we have no idea, but she looks lost and tired. We give her hot, sweet tea and a sandwich. She eats quickly without speaking, all the while dripping rainwater onto our kitchen floor.

We ask for her name, but she doesn't tell us. Looking at her I don't think she can. She looks exhausted.

'I'm so tired,' she says, 'can I sleep here?'

Her eyes are half closed and her head begins to droop.

'Of course you can, love,' says Linda.

'But we need to let your mum know where you are,' I say, 'so just tell us her name and phone number, so we can let her know you're safe.'

She yawns and begins to slide from her chair, eyes half closed.

'That can wait till the morning, surely,' says Linda 'Just look at her, she's exhausted, poor lamb I'll help her up to Julie's room while you lock up.'

Linda has kept Julie's room exactly as it was the day she died, as if ready for her return. She spends some time in there, alone, every day. Sometimes only a few minutes, at other times an hour or more. Often I hear her sobbing to herself. She has made it clear that she wants to be alone in Julie's room, so I don't intrude. I find the room claustrophobic and, although full of memories, unpleasant to be in. I can barely breathe in the room for fear of displacing something and then Linda will be upset and accuse me of not caring about Julie. No one has slept in the room since Julie died. I think it's morbid, but what do I know about a mother's grief. So I leave Linda helping the poor girl into Julie's pyjamas and Julie's bed while I lock up the house for the night.

After she has said goodnight to the girl I try and talk to Linda about phoning the police.

'I'm worn out,' says Linda. 'I need to sleep, can't it wait until the morning?'

Linda quickly falls asleep, something that hasn't happened in over a year. So I convince myself that it can wait until tomorrow.

When I wake Linda is still asleep. She has been waking early, six am. or sometimes five, so I leave her to sleep. I have breakfast alone, and take Linda a cup of tea before I have to leave for work. I look in on Julie's room on the way, and see the dark curly hair of the girl, still fast asleep, on Julie's pillow. Linda gives me a smile as I gently wake her.

'How is she?' she asks.

'Still sleeping. I've got to go to work. Will you ring the police? Call me if you need anything.'

'Don't worry,' she says. 'I'll see to everything, you go off and I'll see you later,' and another smile.

I don't know why but at work everything falls into place. I concentrate easily on the project I'm assigned to, something I've been having trouble doing. Others notice this too.

'It's good to see the old Tom back in the office,' my boss says as I leave at the end of the day.

When I get home the first thing I hear is Linda's laughter. It comes from the kitchen, but fills the whole house. I feel as if a great weight has been lifted from me.

They are both in the kitchen with flour on their hands, and the girl with a smudge on her nose.

'Hello hon,' says Linda, giving me a welcome kiss and a smile. 'Do you want a cup of tea, kettle's boiled'. The girl is wearing some of Julie's old clothes, much too big for her.

'Have you phoned the police?' I say.

'Oh Tom, we've been so busy I completely forgot. We had to wash her clothes, and they're not dry yet, and then we got baking together.'

Linda looks so happy. I get myself a cup of tea and sit down at the kitchen table with them both.

'Somebody, somewhere is missing a daughter and will be really worried about her. We can't ignore this.' I turn to the girl, 'What is your name?'

'I... I... can't remember,' she says. 'I don't know who I am,' and she begins to sob.

'It's been like this all day, Tom, she really can't remember. Don't be hard on her,' says Linda.

'Hey, calm down now, no one's cross with you. Have you got a phone? Shall we look in your school bag?' I ask the girl.

She doesn't have a phone, or any money, and nothing in her pockets that will identify her. The three of us empty her bag onto the kitchen table and pore through the contents. Mainly the sort of text books and hand-outs you would expect from someone in year eight. No names on any of them, except on the back of one of the hand-outs there is a scribbled name, Stephanie Langton, and a landline number.

'Stephanie, is that your name?' I say.

'Stephanie,' she repeats, as if trying it for size. 'Stephanie, Steph, yes Steph, I quite like that, Steph could be my name.'

'Well where do you live, Steph?'

'I don't …don't… know,' and the sobs start again.

'Leave her alone,' Linda says. 'You're frightening her. If that's her name, then that will be her phone number. Why don't you just ring it and speak to her parents?'

A woman answers the phone.

'Is that Mrs Langton?'

'Yes, who's that?'

'Well, you don't know me, but I'm calling about your daughter, Stephanie'

There's an anguished cry at the other end of the phone, followed by a gasp and deep sobbing, then a man's voice.

'Who are you and what do you want?'

'I'm just calling about your daughter, Stephanie'

'You sick bastard. What the hell do you think you're playing at? How did you get this number? My wife has only just begun answering the phone again. If you ever ring this number again I'll have you arrested, unless I get my hands on you first.' And the line goes dead.

A quick internet search tells us that Stephanie Langton was run over and killed by a bus three years ago. There's a picture of Stephanie, a blonde girl about eight years old. She had run into the road while being chased by her mother. The press hounded the bereaved couple for months "investigating" the family argument that preceded the accident. She looks nothing like the girl eating an evening meal with us, but who we are now calling Steph.

'We must contact the authorities,' I say. 'Somebody must have reported her missing.'

I see the conflict inside Linda written on her face. She is enjoying "Steph", enjoying her being in the house, enjoying doing those "mum" things with her. And she doesn't want it to stop. But she knows it can't go on. She knows that what she's enjoying isn't really hers. That Steph has real parents somewhere else who don't deserve to go through what they must be going through.

I wait, and eventually I hear Linda gently say to

Steph, 'We must find out where your parents are so you can go home'

'But I don't want to go anywhere. I like it here.' She's beginning to get upset again.

I wait. Linda takes a breath, and as she exhales the old Linda, the competent, caring, thoughtful Linda, the mother of our child, the Linda I haven't seen for a year, reappears.

'I'm sure your uniform is dry now, why don't you take it to your room and put it away while we make some phone calls,' Linda says. 'I'll be up in a minute to give you hand.'

'Okay,' says Steph, calming down.

'No, there have been no reports of missing girls,' the police officer replies, 'but if you say you've found one I'll ask a family liaison officer to pop round and take a statement.'

When she arrives we recognise her. She is the same officer assigned to us when we lost Julie. She comes in and sits with us and listens patiently to what we have to say. Then she asks to speak to Steph. Linda goes upstairs to fetch her.

'Jim, come quick,' she calls.

Upstairs I find Linda standing in Julie's room alone. Julie's old clothes are folded neatly on the bed. There's a depression in the pillow where a head has been. But of Steph, her school uniform and bag, there is no sign.

The family liaison officer makes some remarks about grief expressing itself in strange ways and asks if we would like to access some counselling.

After she has gone we are again in Julie's room.

Linda looks around the room. 'You know' she says, 'I think it's about time we cleared this room out. I'm sure someone will be grateful for all Julie's old stuff. I don't think I need this anymore.'

I don't show her the long dark hair I find under the pillow as we strip the bed.

Daylight Murder

DAYLIGHT MURDER WAS written during the Covid pandemic when wearing a mask in public was required.

'These are the last two to be had anywhere in town,' said Sergeant Scotty McKenzie as he put on a mask and handed one to his boss, Detective Inspector Guy Farley.

'Better start wheeling them in,' said Guy, donning his own mask.

The murder had been brutal and bloody, but that didn't worry Guy, murder was his speciality. The motive seemed obvious, the victim wore expensive clothes but had no wallet, watch, phone or car keys. The body lay near the last ATM in the town. It should have been easy to solve too, a murder on the high street of a provincial town during market day, there were fifty witnesses.

Scotty introduced them, one after another, into the makeshift interview room. Guy questioned them. From the little old lady buying a few veg to the hotel manager ordering the weeks fresh produce, even the youths trying to hide their forbidden skateboards, they all told the same story.

'There were two of them attacked him with knives. They didn't stop when he fell but carried on. Then one of them rummaged in his pockets taking everything out while the other watched us.'

'What was their hair like?' asked Guy.

'I couldn't say, they wore caps.'

'What about their clothes?'

'I didn't notice. They were covered in blood, it went everywhere.'

'Did you see their faces?'

'Of course not, they were wearing masks.'

They were wearing masks. Of course they were wearing masks, everyone was.

'I could use a pint,' said Sergeant Wade after the last witness had left, 'seeing how the pubs have reopened today.'

'I disapprove of drinking on duty,' said Guy, 'but this time I think I'll join you.'

They went first to The Shepherds Legs Inn. The crowd in the pub were all trying to keep their distance from each other. Scotty headed for the bar, but before he got there, his boss said. 'Not here

Scotty, come on we're leaving.'

'What's wrong with the Shepherds, Guv, it's a good pint?'

'I think we'll do better elsewhere, Scotty.'

It was the same in The Rustic Rover, The Venal Vintner, The Melodious Monk and The Flag and Flutter.

When they got to The Socket and Spanner, Guy said, 'We'll take a table outside, by the door. And we'll just have a half.'

Scotty's face fell. The Socket was renowned for its Steampunk Heavy, one pint could change your view of the world.

They sat for three hours nursing half a pint. The crowd inside became more boisterous. At closing time, they began to stream out.

'Time for action, Scotty,' said Guy. He pointed out two men, 'you take the blonde-haired bloke and I'll take the other.'

After the two had confessed at the station Scotty finally plucked up the courage to ask his boss how he knew it was them.

'This is why you're still a sergeant and I'm the Inspector,' said Guy, 'They were the only people in the whole town without masks.'

Scotty kicked himself, of course the masks came off, all that blood was a dead giveaway.

The Rusty Nail

'WHAT HAVE YOU found?' Jeanette's words were whipped away by the wind and never reached her husband's ears. She caught up with Mark, crouching on the shingle, examining his latest find.

'What is it?' she said, a little breathless.

'It's only a big old rusty nail. I feel like someone out of "The Detectorists", never getting to do the Dance of Gold.'

Jeanette laughed. Beachcombing was a common pastime since buying their cottage by the sea, and although they were not equipped with metal detectors, they had sharp eyes. They had never found anything of value, and now they had decided to sell the cottage they hoped for a 'special' find on what would be one of their last trips to the beach.

'At least you've found something,' said Jeanette,

as the wind and spray blew fiercely.

'And something I can easily carry home,' said Mark, slipping the nail into his pocket, and promptly forgetting it. They turned back to the cottage where their son, David, would be making coffee.

'You know you don't need to do this,' said David, helping them off with their coats.

'We've talked it over many times, David, it's what we want to do. We've had some good years here, but now we want to help as much as we can. So we'll sell the cottage. It's simple.'

And it would help, David didn't deny that. Since the tragedy that left David bringing up twin infant sons alone, life had become financially difficult. Industrial Archaeology, David's passion and recent employment, did not make for a lavish lifestyle.

'Well thanks both of you, I really don't know what to say. I think I need a walk. Can you watch the twins for me?'

'It's just started raining look, borrow your dad's coat.'

'I'm really going to miss this old place,' said Jeanette after David had left. 'I was really looking forward to holidays here with the twins, they would love it when they're older.'

'I know, but we're doing the right thing. David needs the money now.'

The door pushed open and the wind and rain

blew in David, soaking wet and holding the rusty nail in his hand. 'What's this Dad? Where did you get it?'

'Just a rusty old nail I found on the beach; I'd forgotten about it.'

'But look here, dad.' On the head of the nail were the corroded remnants of letters and numbers.

'This isn't a nail dad, it's a rivet! You can just make out an R, and a T, and a 4. I think this is a 401 rivet. They were used on the Titanic.'

Later the rusty nail went to auction. It had been dated and authenticated as being part of the Titanic itself. Speculation suggested it might have been one of the 'faulty' rivets that caused the ship to sink. The hammer fell at £650,000.

That evening, back at the cottage, they all performed the 'Dance of Gold' passing the twins between them.

Shelter From the Storm

I HATE THIS kind of rain; it reminds me of that day when I had just turned sixteen.

It was a Tuesday. A Tuesday in June. You told me you weren't doing anything much that day and I could call and see you if I wished. You knew I wished very much to come and call on you, you knew I had been hoping to see you alone for months. I showered and washed my hair and dressed as well as I could and set off for your house. I had to catch two buses and then walk the half mile length of the lane you lived in.

Eventually I arrived, smoothed down my hair and rang your doorbell.

'Tina? She's not here, love. Gone into town with some friends, she'll be out all day. I don't expect to see her before five.' Your mother had a kind voice and looked at me as if she knew I had been fooled.

I didn't accept the drink she offered. I found myself being upset, lost, angry all at once.

I held it together to give what I hoped was a sincere sounding apology and turned to walk the four miles home. The heavens opened when I was about fifty yards from your garden gate, and I was soaked to the skin by the time I got to the end of the lane.

I was about a mile from town when I met you coming the other way. The rain hiding my tears, I could almost ignore you but you caught my eye.

'What are you doing here, Jamie?' you said, as if you didn't know.

But I didn't answer you. I didn't speak to you that day. I walked on past. My sixteen-year-old pride was not so destroyed by you that I would give you any sort of explanation while you were in the company of Ron. Both of you sheltering under his raincoat. Probably the only person in the world who would carry a raincoat in June.

The next day you came to see me at school. You wanted to talk. You were conciliatory. Wanted to make up. I said no. I stood my ground. I held my head high. I wouldn't be friends.

'Go and chat up boring Ron, he's your type, just leave me alone.' I said. I hated myself as I spoke. I hated Ron, I wanted you, I loved you.

But you went to Ron. You married him instead of me, had his children.

Yes, I know it was a long time ago, fifty-two years ago next week. Yes, I know it was stupid. Yes, I know we were kids. But here we both are, sheltering from the same rain under this tree. Where's Ron's raincoat now? Buried with him you say. I'm sorry about that. But I'm not as stupid as I was then, so will you dance in the rain with me? Yes, at our age.

Shopping Trip

I SAID I would drop her by the bridge at the bottom of High Street. It was our weekly shopping trip into town, and she had been hankering after a new cushion for her chair, to ease her back, like. So before I park the car, I leave her down by that furniture place, you know, Suites and Beds 'R' Us.

'I'll meet you at our usual coffee place,' I say.

'Alright love,' she says, 'see you in about an hour.'

Well, I'm a bloke, aren't I? It never takes an hour to do a bit of shopping, so I'm in the coffee shop ahead of time. I have a coffee and read the free newspaper. Then I have another and read another newspaper. Now she's late, but no more than usual. I don't want any more coffee, so I just sit and watch the world go by. Young mums with their tots come in for coffee and stay while the little ones behave. Some people are sat with computers. I don't know what they are doing. Maybe working? But I don't know what sort of work that would be.

That sets me to thinking about work. It's been ten years since I retired, but I can't say as I miss it much. But it gives us a bit of a pension. Not a lot, but enough to get by on.

But where is she? She's an hour late now and I'm getting worried. I hope she hasn't had one of the dizzy spells she's been getting lately. And she's always tired. She says she gets dizzy because she's tired, but I don't know. I think there's something wrong. I hope she hasn't fallen over. She'd be so upset if she embarrassed herself like that in public.

I head down the high street looking for her. I can see a gaggle of folk up ahead and wonder if she's there, but it's only kids, admiring a new phone one of them has. I don't know what all that fuss is about mobile phones, I can't be bothered with them.

I look in the other cafes in case she's gone in the wrong one, but she hasn't. I look in the charity shops too, in case she's gone looking for a new book, but she isn't there either. I'm really worried now.

Then I'm at the bottom of High Street and I haven't seen her. I go into Suites and Beds 'R' Us. It's my last hope.

'Can I help you?' says the lass behind the

counter.

'I don't think so,' I say, 'I've lost my wife.'

'Come with me,' she says. I follow her round the displays of furniture. And there she is! She's fast asleep on one of those recliner things, with her feet up. She looks ever so peaceful.

'It seemed such a shame to disturb her,' says the lass.

'I don't care how much, we'll have it,' I say.

Special Delivery

THIS STORY WAS written at the height of the Covid Pandemic.

'What is the matter with you? You know you have to go out and deliver,' said Mrs Claus.

'It's different this year, it doesn't feel the same. I look down south and all I see is sickness and disease. It looks pretty horrible.'

'You've seen worse, remember? Or are you getting a bit old for this job?' Mrs Claus always knew the right thing to say to fire up her rotund husband and get him moving.

'Too old! Of course I'm not too old. I feel as fit as when I was two hundred.'

'What is it then? Look, here's a nice cup of cocoa. Tell me what's really troubling you?'

Santa took off his big red jacket, slipped off his

braces and sat in his huge chair before the giant log fire in the Claus's sitting room.

'To be honest with you my love,' he began, 'to be honest, I'm scared.'

First Mrs Claus laughed, thinking he was joking. He'd never been scared of anything, as far as she could remember. But he was serious in his look.

'What is it your scared of,' she said softly.

'I'm scared of the Horrid Coviddy thingy. They say the older you are the more dangerous it is. And there isn't anyone older than me, except perhaps Methuselah, but he never goes anywhere so he's alright.'

'But my dearest, the children have to get their presents, you promised when you took the job.'

'I know, but what if I get the Horrid Coviddy and succumb. Next year no one will get any presents.'

'But don't you deliver in the deep dark night when all the younglings are abed and asleep?'

'Yeeesss,' said Santa, not sure what Mrs Clause was getting at.

'And isn't the Horrid Coviddy caught from people when they kiss and hug and talk and cough and sneeze near each other?'

'Yeeesss'.

'Then you needn't be worried. They are all far away in the Land of Nod when you visit.'

Santa mulled this over as he drained his cocoa. 'You're right,' he said, brightening. Then a cloud came over him again.

'Sometimes, the glass of something special that's been left for me looks like someone may have taken a sip. I might catch it then. And if I don't drink the glass, children won't think I've been and will stop believing in me.'

'That is serious,' said Mrs Claus, deep in thought. 'What you need is a special Christmas Card to take with you telling the children you've given up drinking. If you leave that behind, they'll know you've been.'

'But it's one of the perks of the job,' said a crestfallen Santa.

'One I've long thought you should have given up on, and now's the perfect opportunity.'

So on Christmas morning, if you find a card from Santa and a full glass untouched, you know he's been down your chimney. But if you find an empty glass, just don't tell Mrs Claus or he'll be in trouble.

The Birthday Gift

'You shouldn't have, I told you not to get me anything.'

We were in a restaurant having a celebratory meal.

'It's a birthday present, you're supposed to say thank you and tell me how thoughtful I am,' she said.

Margaret was clearly upset. I had definitely said the wrong thing, and she was right, it had been crass of me. She had taken time to go and find me a present, wrap it up and wait until my birthday to give it to me. The least I could do would be to have the grace to accept it.

'I'm sorry, you're right, I'm being an oaf, thank you, darling, you are truly kind. And thoughtful.' I took the parcel from her. By the size and weight, it was clearly a book, a hardback of generous proportions. I have always loved reading. I'm one of those people who believe you can never have enough books.

I'm old enough to savour moments like this and don't rush to tear the paper open. First, I inspect the parcel. It has been expertly wrapped, Sellotape binding each perfectly formed envelope end, and sealing the centre join. The challenge between us, whenever gifts are exchanged, is to open the packet without damaging the paper. Initially this was so expensive wrapping could be reused, a necessary expedient during our young family days when cash was hard to come by. Now it was a ritual of delayed gratification, the aim to remove all the Sellotape without disclosing the contents of the package. It took me ten minutes, but there it sat, intact and still completely covered in wrapping but without a trace of Sellotape.

During this we talked. I told her again, how much I enjoyed reading and that books were always a welcome gift.

'Any kind of book?' she said.

'Yes, any kind. I'm always interested in reading styles I've never read before.'

'Well, I'm certain you've never read a book like this before.'

'Certain is a big word, how can you be so sure?'

'Well, you've never read one like this while I've known you. In fact, I don't think you've ever opened a book like this. Yet there are thousands out there. They are hugely popular and sell in millions.'

My curiosity was piqued, and I almost scrabbled the parcel open to see what great literary genre I had been missing out on but paused to again express my effusive thanks.

'Darling, you are the most kind and thoughtful of women. It has been a great honour and pleasure to have shared these last thirty-five years with you.' I gave her my most generous and intimate smile and picked up the book, still encased in its sky-blue wrapping.

Slowly I unfolded the paper to reveal the mystery inside. She was right. I had never read anything like "Cooking – For Men Who Won't". I looked at her determined expression and immediately resolved to absorb and utilise the entire contents of this gift.

The Last Battle

JASPHAREN STOOD, PANTING, at the edge of the vast plain, knowing that his struggle was not yet over. There would be one more battle to fight before victory could be his.

He renewed his grip on Scrythe, the magical sword that had delivered the final blow to many of his enemies. As he stepped onto the plain, he heard the sound for the first time. Was it a voice? Calling his name? He was unsure but he knew that Vaxten, his mortal enemy, would do anything to defeat him. Even sending wraiths and ghouls to distract him from the quest.

It felt like many months since Jaspharen had begun this journey. The route from his citadel was marked by the fallen bodies of his enemies. Now but one remained. Jaspharen needed only to defeat Vaxten and victory would be his. But first he must cross the wilderness to reach Vaxten's stronghold.

Again, the sound came to him 'Jaspharen... Jaspharen' as if carried on the wind from a far corner of the world.

'I must remain resolute,' he told himself as he began to jog across the deserted landscape. As far as the eye could see there was but desert. The only sign that man had ever been there were the bleached bones of those who had failed in the quest. Jaspharen was resolved that he would not be joining them.

Then the voice again, from behind him in a breathless whisper scudding over the desert. 'Jaspharen... Jaspharen... come, come to me.' He turned but could see nothing and no one. Trickery, he must not succumb. He turned back to his journey and began to run, feet pounding on the desert floor.

As he ran the spires and turrets of his enemy's castle appeared on the horizon. He slowed to a walk. He needed to conserve energy for this last battle. Again the voice came from behind, calling him. 'Jaspharen, come, now, now.' It was louder and clearer. He almost turned towards it but resolved to remain focused on the quest. His fortitude paid off, for at that moment he saw the huge gates of the castle open.

As Jaspharen's mighty foe stepped through the gates it felt as if the ground shuddered beneath him. 'Don't fail me, courage,' Jaspharen murmured as he marched, steadfastly towards his nemesis.

'Jaspharen! Come! Now!' the voice was insistent, but so was the gleam in Vaxten's eye. Jaspharen raised his sword and began to charge, as did his foe.

As their swords clashed for the first time, throwing sparks and blinding thunder flashes across the desert floor, Jaspharen heard the crash behind him and felt the heat of breath on his collar. He turned.

'Jasper, if you don't come and have your tea now, I'll ban you from the internet for a month.' His mother stomped from the bedroom. As Jasper went to comply, he caught a glimpse of the screen. His hero lay dead on the sand as 'Game Over' flashed red.

A Visit to Santa

'WHERE ARE WE going, mum?' said Emily.

'I'm taking you to see Santa, I told you I would.'

'Hooray, hooray, hooray.' Emily danced around the kitchen. It's hard to contain excitement when you're five years old.

'Did your mum take you to see him when you were little?' said Emily.

'She did, and I think I was almost as excited as you. And I never forgot what he told me.'

'What did he tell you, mum?'

Julia remembered, word for word, the long-ago conversation. 'That's a secret,' she said. And she would not tell despite Emily's most plaintive pleading.

Mother and daughter arrived at Santa's Grotto and joined the queue of excited children.

As they inched towards the head of the queue

the excited hubbub was replaced by uncertain anticipation.

'What's he like, Santa?' said Emily, nervousness crossing her brow.

'He's very wise, and very kind,' said Julia.

Emily stayed quiet until it was her turn. The Elf took Emily by the hand and led mother and daughter into the Grotto. There, bedecked in red with a huge white beard and bright blue sparkling eyes, sat the same man Julia had seen all those years ago.

'Ho, ho, ho, you must be Emily,' he boomed.

'But, how do you know?' a quiet Emily said.

'I know all the children, and all those who used to be children,' and he looked at Emily's mother.

'Hello Dr Julia, I hope you are well. You have a beautiful daughter. But please stand back. As you know the conversation between Emily and I must be secret.'

As Julia stepped back Santa began to talk quietly with Emily.

'What would you like to be when you grow up, Emily?'

'I want to be a princess,' said Emily.

'Then I am certain you shall be,' said Santa.

Emily looked doubtful. 'Are you sure?'

'Oh yes, very sure. If that is what you really want to be. But here's a secret. You can change your mind if you want to. People often change their mind as they get a bit older. You might decide you want to be an explorer, or an astronaut, then you will be one. All you have to do is tell yourself that's what you really want to be.'

'I don't have to do anything else, just tell myself?' said Emily.

'There may be other things to do, but they'll be easy. The first thing is to tell yourself. Now here's another secret. When your mother was your age, she wanted to be a ballerina.'

'But she isn't one,' said Emily, a little too loudly.

'Well, she changed her mind when she was ten, and decided she wanted to be a doctor.'

'And she is a doctor,' said Emily incredulously, 'it really does work.'

On the drive home Julia said, 'did you have a good visit with Santa?'

'Oh, yes,' said Emily, 'I told him I wanted to be a princess when I grow up. But I may change my mind later.'

Julia smiled.

The Resolution

'YOU NEED TO take more exercise, Dad.'

I'd heard it before, not only from my daughter but the doctor as well. I just couldn't be bothered. I knew why. It was since I lost Susan. We used to walk a lot during our forty years together, but now it just wasn't the same. But to shut my daughter up I agreed to start walking again in the new year.

'A new year's resolution,' I said, 'I'll have a walk twice a week. Now can we get on with enjoying ourselves?'

She waited until the 2nd of January to ring and remind me of the resolution. It seemed a fine day, so I told her I was just about to go out.

Where I live it's rural and the walks are lovely, but not short. I talked myself into a walk up the hill, down the other side, then back to the pub for refreshment.

I didn't see a soul until after I'd crowned the hill and begun my descent. Then I saw a figure below me, heading uphill. It looked like it would be ten minutes before we met. But after a little while I saw the person stumble, then slip off the path and begin to fall down the hill side. I chuckled to myself, thinking they must have slipped, but then I saw the figure lying still on the grass.

Something's wrong, I thought and quickened my pace. I was out of breath when I found the unconscious woman.

I'd done some first aid long ago so checked for vital signs, breaks and bleeding. There wasn't much to see, but she didn't look like she was coming round. I couldn't carry her down the hill, it was more than I could manage, and she clearly needed help. Then it started raining, heavily.

I phoned the emergency services, and ten minutes later the Air Ambulance was hovering overhead. They winched her aboard and then said, 'you'd better come along too.' The crew had her on a drip by the time I was onboard, and they took us to hospital.

I didn't even know her name, but the staff kept telling me about her, how she was all right and would be able to go home soon.

Then, there she was, thanking me for saving her life. It turns out she was diabetic and had forgotten to bring any sugar with her on her walk. If the ambulance hadn't got to her, she would have died.

I got us a taxi home, least I could do.

'What were you doing, walking in this weather?' I said in the back of the taxi.

'Well, it was fine when I set off,' she said, 'and I'd promised my son I'd get more exercise, a sort of new year's resolution.'

She didn't understand why I laughed, but we've been walking together for a year now. And whenever we walk, we count our miles and contribute to the Air Ambulance. We both know neither of us would be walking without them.

The Special Date

Jason was ambitious and hardworking. Not only that, but he was also good at what he did. But he had only been with the Estate Agency about a year, so he was surprised when his boss, the Branch Manager, invited him to attend the Chamber of Commerce annual dinner. Jason did not think it would be up to much as a social occasion but the opportunities for networking were not to be missed.

As Jason squeezed into his seat in the packed banquet hall his chair bumped against another behind him. He turned to apologise, and his eyes met Claire's. The din of the room faded as he took in the beauty before him. They hardly spoke to anyone else the entire evening and by the end of the night Jason and Claire had arranged to go out together.

They dated and got on well. The more they met the more they liked each other. Anyone seeing them together could not help but smile and think that here were two people just made for each other. It seemed to Jason that Claire was really special, and by the way she acted he guessed she felt the same about him.

'I'd like to take you on a special lunch date,' Jason told Claire one day, 'on Sunday.'

'Okay,' said Claire, beguiled by the air of mystery surrounding Jason's request.

Jason picked her up that Sunday at noon.

'Where are we going then, Mr. Mysterious?' asked Claire.

'It's a surprise,' said Jason, in his best mysterious voice.

Jason drove them out of town for a couple of miles to of a large private house, hidden behind an ancient yew hedge. Claire saw that the 'For Sale' sign at the entrance to the drive had been marked 'Sale Agreed'.

Jason turned into the long, private drive and pulled up in front of the porch. He took a set of keys from his pocket and opened the imposing front door. 'Come on in, Claire,' he said, shyly.

Claire giggled as she followed Jason into the expensive property. 'You're going to pull the old Estate Agent trick and have your wicked way with me in the master bedroom, aren't you?' said Claire.

'I sincerely hope not, my dear,' said Jason's mother as she entered the hall from the kitchen, 'I think it's just lunch you'll be having today.'

Claire's embarrassment was vivid.

Jason's father, following on behind, struggled to keep a straight face. 'You might at least wait until the property's empty, son,' he said. A broad grin spread over his face as he looked at Claire's flushed face. 'You must be Claire. I think a glass of red wine would suit you very well, come on through.'

The two couples, for that was what they were, laughed together throughout a successful 'meet the parents' lunch.

The Trip of a Lifetime

WHEN MARJORIE HAD said they weren't getting any younger and if Sheila wanted to fulfil her lifelong ambition, she'd better get on with it, it galvanised Sheila into action and they started planning.

Marjorie had never understood Sheila's obsession with the Hanging Gardens of Babylon but was happy to join her decades old friend in an adventure.

They scrimped and saved every penny, going without all the small treats they had during the year, their weekly cup of tea at 'Ye Olde Oak Tea Rooms', the small glass of sherry on a Saturday while watching 'Strictly'.

They just managed to save enough for a very off-season trip, with economy flights. But that didn't detract from the growing excitement. Every week before the departure date they took turns providing tea and a bun in lieu of a trip to Ye Olde Oak. And each week Marjorie would leave Shiela in stitches as they talked about what might befall during their trip. Marjorie's description of how they would foil a hijack attempt on the plane with artful use of knitting needles sent Sheila scurrying to the smallest room in fits of laughter. Her depiction of holiday romances with romantic camel herders had a similar impact.

It was a bitter January day when the two left the taxi at Stanstead to board their flight to Babylon.

'It must be minus ten,' said Sheila, 'it won't be this cold in Iraq, will it?'

'No, it never gets below freezing there, if it did the camels… humps would fall off,' said Marjorie. Her pause before 'humps' setting Sheila off laughing again.

Once settled in the cheap hotel the two took a taxi out to the Hanging Gardens.

It was undeniable that the terraces of mud brick were enormous, stretching high into the pale winter sky, and that they were numerous, uncountable, was obvious. But greenery and colour were notable by their absence rather than profligacy. A few grey stumps protruded here and there from the grey soil and the grey walls. No flowers, no ferns, no foliage at all. It looked like nothing had grown there for centuries.

'Is that it then?' said Sheila.

'I guess it must be,' said Marjorie.

'I thought it would be, you know, a bit more…'

'Spectacular,' added Marjorie.

'Yes, spectacular.'

'Verdant,' said Marjorie.

'Yes, verdant,' said Sheila, a hesitancy in her voice.

Marjorie looked at her friend and saw her on the verge of tears. Her disappointment absolute.

'It looks more like a desert than a garden,' said Sheila, her voice cracking.

'But you know, Sheila,' said Marjorie, making sure Sheila turned to look at her, 'it probably looks at its best in the spring.'

Sheila looked at her friend for a moment then burst into her characteristic laugh.

'You're right, come on, let's go home. We're bound to get a free cuppa at the Olde Oak when we tell them.'

'And we can get some duty-free sherry too,' said Marjorie, to more accompanying laughter.

A Work of Fiction

'I DON'T UNDERSTAND.'

'It's really simple,' she says, 'just change the bits I've underlined, put in the bits I've suggested, and it'll be perfect. The piece will go out with your name under the headline. You'll have made it onto the front page of a national newspaper, your career in journalism is made. What don't you understand?'

'If I make these changes, it affects the whole meaning of the piece. It emphasises something that isn't important, takes attention away from the real story which is…'

'Yes, yes, I know what the 'real' story is, but we can't make those sorts of allegations in the Daily Bugle, the owners wouldn't stand for it. Besides, do you remember what the assignment was when you went undercover at the factory?'

'They aren't allegations, these things did happen. And yes, I remember the assignment was to report on how migrant workers were taking jobs away from the local people, but…'

'And when you make these changes, you'll have completed the assignment, so just get on with it, we have a deadline to make.'

The editor gives me a quick stern look then deliberately pulls out some other journo's work, signalling the end of our conversation. I get up to leave. As I open her door her voice penetrates the press office hubbub.

'I want to see the final version on my desk by three this afternoon. Don't let me down with this Jason.'

'Okay Rebecca, I'll get right on it,' I say. I'm busy thinking how I might word the piece to salvage some of the tragic tale of greed and exploitation I had uncovered.

'This won't do.'

I'm again in Rebecca's office. It is now three fifteen. Her baleful glare ensures there is no doubt about her mood.

'I know what you've done. You can't slip these things past me. We are clear about this whole immigration issue. If you can't see the problem in the same way, we can do without your talents. I have an alternative leader for tomorrow.'

'It doesn't feel honest. These people are paid half the minimum wage and have most of that deducted for pitifully substandard accommodation. They really are the victims here.'

'It's your choice. Do it and do it now or clear your desk and get out. We haven't room for namby-pamby, lefty ideals in this organisation.'

What do I do? Do I stick to my ideals and insist on the truth, or do I make the changes asked, and although the piece would not be all lies, it wouldn't give the full picture either? When you see the Bugle on the newsstands tomorrow, you'll know. If the headline is 'Paedo's in Paradise' I've stuck to my principles but lost my job. If it's 'Doomed to the Dole' I've sold out but can still feed my family. Either way, the piece beneath the headline will be a work of fiction.

Seating Arrangements

'IT'LL BE EASY, I don't know why you're making such an issue over it.'

'It won't be easy I tell you. You think that everything's easy and you don't plan anything, but you can't just leave everything to chance. You want it to be a success, don't you?'

'Well yes of course, but....'

'Then we need to plan it. We are only going to get one chance to do this.'

'Yes, yes, I know all this, but I still don't see why every detail has to be decided in advance, why can't people just sit where they want?'

'What about you, where are you going to sit?'

'At the front, of course, next to....'

'And suppose someone else gets there first and sits at the front, where will you sit then?'

'That's different. Of course I'll be at the front,

everybody will know that.'

'Will they? How will they know? What about people who've come a long way to see this? How will they know they aren't supposed to sit at the front?'

'I don't know why you always make things difficult. This will be easy, trust me. I will sit up front and everybody else can find their own seats.'

'And what about me? Where am I going to sit?'

'Next to me, like I said.'

'You didn't say.'

'I would have said if you hadn't interrupted. Look what is the problem with this, we turn up, sit down, do the deed, and leave, what's so complicated?'

'That's the trouble with you, you make out that things are really easy, you never put any thought into the planning and organisation, and then, when everything works out fine, you take all the credit for the 'big idea', and you never mention anybody else's efforts at all.'

'What are you talking about? I don't know what you mean.'

'For instance, remember your mother's eightieth birthday?'

'Of course I do, what a great night that was, everybody enjoyed themselves. You've got to admit that was a great idea. And it was easy. Even you enjoyed yourself.'

'It was easy, was it? Do you remember how many people were there?'

'Yes, of course, eighty, like we planned.'

'Ha! I like the 'planned', and the 'we'. Yes, there were eighty people there like you suggested. Do you remember why there weren't seventy-nine, or how we nearly had eighty-one?'

'We only invited eighty, that's why there were eighty people there, stop being so daft about this.'

'You exasperate me, you really do. The reason why there was exactly eighty people there was because muggins here made sure that everybody would be there by ringing them the day before and having a couple of extra 'invitees' to fill in for your wretched cousin and her drip of a husband who pulled out at the last minute.'

'There's no need to…'

'And it was me who had to tell the sixteen people who wanted to come but weren't invited because it would spoil the 'purity' of your idea.'

'Who?'

'Well, there was Jim and Margaret from the lunch club, known her for fifteen years, Alice and her daughter who your mother befriended at the drop-in, Caroline her cleaner…'

'Yes, yes all right, I didn't realise so many people wanted to come, maybe we could have done it twice.'

'You didn't realise, that just about sums it up,

you never realise how much effort goes into these things.'

'Look I'm sorry, for whatever, but I still don't know why we need a seating plan.'

'It's like this, you know your uncle Bob?'

'Yes....'

'Where do you think he'll be for the hour or two before the ceremony?'

'Ha, that's easy, knowing Uncle Bob he'll be in the pub.'

'And when he comes in who do you think he'll want to sit next to?'

'Ah. Yes well, he'll try and make a beeline for whoever is the prettiest young woman in the room of course, but I can ask Mark to keep an eye out for him and put him at the back of the room.'

'You can't ask Mark to be responsible for where the argumentative old sod sits, have you completely lost your mind. What will Bob do if Mark tells him to sit at the back? It will be loud and offensive, he might even take a swing at Mark. You are really going to dump this on your best friend? Doesn't he already have enough to do?'

'All right I see what you mean, someone else can see to Bob.'

'No they can't, there isn't anyone else.'

'Could you...'

'No, no, no, a thousand times no. I am not going to be subjected to the obnoxious pawing of that evil old letch. And I'll be too busy. There's another reason for a seating plan.'

'What?'

'Do you really think my family and friends are going to want to sit next to yours.'

'Why not? Everything's friendly isn't it? We are agreed on this aren't we? We decided long ago that if it ever came to...'

'It's friendly between you and me, but do you really expect my family to see it in the same way? What about my Aunt Dora? You know she's a...'

'Okay, okay, I get the message, your snobby family don't want to mix with the lowlife that is mine. They always were a priggish bunch, and that Dora, well if I had my way...'

'There is no need to be insulting about my family. This really is too much. Who can blame them if they behave like Bob, I mean...'

'They don't all behave like Uncle Bob, that's not fair.'

'Look, we are just getting into a row, and we will never settle this, I can't see how we can do this without a seating plan, not if it's going to run smoothly without causing offence to anyone. Think about what it will be like at the end of the ceremony, who will be talking to who.'

'Hmmm, yes, I hadn't thought about after the end. I guess it will be different from the last time we all got together.'

'Yes, vastly different, and we do want to avoid situation where people may decide to express how they feel about the other's family. We don't really know what they think do we? This is precisely why we are having separate receptions.'

'Okay, I see what you mean, but does it need to be a formal seating plan? Couldn't we just have your family on one side, and mine on the other?'

'We could, and I would be fine with my family in that scenario, so if you can cope with your cousins Tom and Mike and their respective partners dealing calmly with the bigotry of Vince and Elsie that's fine.'

'To be honest, I don't think my lot would take any notice of a seating plan, but they could understand your family is on the left and mine on the right.'

'Then wording of the invitation is right.'

As an attendee at the wedding of Ellen and Jamie
You are cordially invited to celebrate their
Divorce and Separation at a ceremony on July 24th.
Seating arrangements:
Bride to the left
Groom to the right
Separate receptions will be held in the evening at
secret locations to be disclosed following the
ceremony.

Bus Fare

The old minibus rattled slowly along stopping at every village and hamlet in the valley. It took an interminable two and a half hours to make the journey from the head of the valley to the terminus in the small market town, where the driver would have his lunch before making the return trip.

Phil, the bus driver for over twenty years, lived on his own in a small cottage at the head of the valley. He had enough space to park the bus overnight, a boon to both Phil and the bus company as it meant they could cut the service up and down the valley to a single bus a day, arguing with the local community that an hour in town was sufficient to do any business they had there. Phil was a bit more flexible with the hour, and the timetable he was supposed to adhere to. He often left the terminus half an hour or more later than scheduled. But as nobody complained to the bus company, they did nothing about it. It also meant that Phil had time to visit Betty Scrogler.

Betty had been Phil's childhood passion at the village school, but since she moved to the metropolis of Goddersdyke, population six thousand and seven, she had become beguiled by the bright lights of high living. Still, she welcomed a visit from Phil every now and again, especially around month end when Phil got paid.

One morning, Phil was surprised, and a little put out, when Betty boarded his bus at a stop just outside Haltingstone, population eight hundred and sixteen, one of the bigger villages along his route.

'What are you doing here, Betty?' said Phil.

'I hope I'm catching a bus on its way to Goddersdyke,' said Betty.

'Alright, no need for sarcasm, but I don't often see you out this way, except when you used to come up...'

'That was a long time ago and no need to bring it up now, Phil. Just do the driving will you,' said Betty.

'That'll be four pounds fifty,' said Phil.

'Four pounds fifty? Whatever for?' said Betty.

'The bus fare, it's four pounds fifty.'

'Bus fare! I've never paid bus fare in my life, and I don't intend to start now,' said Betty, her voice beginning to rise.

The other three passengers already on the bus perked up on hearing this and busily looked elsewhere while focusing entirely on the entertainment they suspected was about to begin.

'It's the rules, Betty. I have to collect a fare from every passenger who boards.'

'I bet it just ends up in the Kings Arms, and if you're not careful they'll be the only arms you'll be seeing the way you're going.'

One of the other passengers converted a quick snigger into exaggerated coughing.

Phil gave him a sidelong look before speaking again. In a barely audible whisper he said, 'This lunchtime then?'

'Give a girl a chance to recover,' said Betty, 'how about tomorrow?'

Phil nodded his agreement and Betty took a seat, her purse intact.

Leave Taking

After thirty years, Carole is leaving the village. She's holding open house for anyone who wants to say goodbye.

I'm in her sitting room drinking cheap instant coffee. There's a knoll sofa, antique armchairs, dining chairs. Odd seats gathered from throughout the house are arranged in a rough circle, some low tables between them. Though full of chairs, many occupied, the room is empty.

The curtains have been taken down. Some of the furniture has gone, sold.

'I don't need so much now...' she leaves the sentence unfinished, makes more unpalatable coffee.

What personal effects remain wait for "the packers" to arrive.

'They do everything,' says Carole, 'they pack it

all up, take it to the new place and unpack. I don't have to do a thing.'

We all mumble our approval. Nobody says, 'why allow strangers to pack your stuff?' We all say, 'what a good idea, that makes sense.'

Perhaps it does make sense. Maybe Carole doesn't want to find a relic, a piece of him she's forgotten that will expose her fragile façade, plunge her into the nadir of grief. So someone else will pack, clear the house of its contents. And then she'll go, leaving nothing, yet everything, behind.

People drift in and out through the afternoon. Some I half recognise, some are strangers, some I regard as friends. They see me when they come in, greet me, ask how I am in that 'I don't really want to know' way, being polite. I return their politeness. What else is there to say?

Sunlight pours through the naked windows, glints on floating dust motes, bounces from polished floorboards. No one takes photos. If someone did it would seem happy, friends greeting each other, shaking hands, hugging, kissing, chattering. But the atmosphere is thin as a mountain top. The talk is small, inconsequential. No one mentions the person who left a year ago, though we all watched Carole throw that first handful of soil. Now people smile that thin, mouth only smile that says, 'I'm smiling,' nothing more. The smile that doesn't say, 'I'll miss you, I wish you were staying.'

I watch Carole. She's efficient, friendly, seemingly cheerful. My head is full of questions that can't be asked. How does she know this is the right time to leave? Does she still talk to him? Wonder why he's late home? Listen for his voice singing in the empty shower? How many tears has she shed? How often does she think of him? Does she have regrets, things left unsaid? Does she cry, at night, alone in the desert of her unshared bed? Does she really have it all under control?

I leave and walk home, turn the key in the lock. I step in and call your name. It's automatic, I do it every time I come home, even though you haven't been here for months. When will I leave? 'Not yet, not yet, not yet,' murmurs the house. I weep selfish tears.

The Performance

Such was the demand for the best seats that people began arriving half an hour before the performance was to start. They queued in the dark and the rain before the doors opened.

The auditorium was full of hustle and bustle as the audience found their seats. There was no seating plan, so people sat wherever they liked. The early arrivals took their favourite spots, some up close in the front rows, some near the back. Many took aisle seats which meant lots of standing and sitting as later arrivals threaded their way into the vacant seats mid row. John and Melanie were two of those late comers, almost last to arrive they had to scan the rows to find a vacant pair of seats.

After the health and safety announcement about fire escapes, the lights dimmed and an expectant hush settled over the gathered throng.

'Is it a long performance?' whispered John.

'The usual length, why?' said Melanie.

'No reason,' said John. Settling back into his seat he pulled a book from inside his jacket and opened it at the marked page.

'What are you doing,' hissed Melanie as actors began to fill the stage.

'Well, I know the story, so I thought I'd catch up on some...' several people made "hushing" sounds in the seats behind the couple and John stopped. He read the expression on his wife's face and closed the book, returning it to his jacket pocket.

At the interval Melanie let John know exactly how she felt about him reading during the performance.

'What's the point of coming if you're not going to watch it?' she said. 'I might as well have come on my own.'

John attempted appeasement. 'You're right, Mel, I'm sorry. It was stupid of me. It's just that...'

Before John could explain himself, the audience were called back for the second act.

'And just make sure you leave that book where it belongs,' said Melanie as they regained their seats.

At the end of the second act the applause was long and vigorous. John and Melanie both joined in with enthusiastic clapping. Then, after a few words of thanks from the director, the audience filed outside once again.

'At least it's stopped raining,' said John as they mingled with the after-show crowd, none in a hurry to depart. 'Do you think she'll be long?'

'No, I don't expect so, look there she is looking for us,' and Mel waved her arms and began calling, 'over here Sophie, over here.' Sophie ran over to join them.

'Did you enjoy it mum, did you see, was I good?' said Sophie.

'I did see you, you were very good,' said Melanie taking hold of her seven-year-old's hand.

'Did you like it dad?' said Sophie, slipping her hand into her fathers and swinging happily between her parents.

'I loved it,' said John, 'you were the best "Mary" I've seen.'

His daughter beamed up at John while the words "this year" remained in his head, unspoken.

Starting Over

The two men met in the back room of the quiet coffee shop.

The elder arrived first. To the casual observer he would have appeared about seventy, maybe seventy-five years old, wearing a smart blazer that might have been new a decade ago and sporting white hair and an unkempt beard. He ordered a black americano and sat in the quietest spot of the café. He waited for his son to appear and wasn't surprised that he was late.

The old man had almost finished his coffee when he heard the café door open and in bounded his son, all enthusiasm. Converse trainers supporting jeans and a denim jacket spoke his determination to remain youthful, but the lines in his face put him in his mid-thirties.

The old man sighed as his son ordered a

cappuccino and a toasted teacake then changed his mind to a mocha and a muffin.

'You're late,' grumbled the old man.

'Yeah, sorry, been busy you know. Do you want another coffee? I'll get it.'

He was halfway out of his seat when the old man said 'no, I don't want anymore. Caffeine plays havoc with my waterworks.'

'What do you think of the project?' said the younger, taking a bite of his muffin.

'You want my honest opinion? It's shite, utter ordure, the excrement of a particularly foul animal that dines exclusively on the rotting entrails of long dead skunk, that's what it is.'

'I think it's going well. People are happy, the sun is shining, there's loads going on. Exciting times, it seems. Don't they say, "may you live in interesting times" and it sure seems interesting to me.'

'That simplistic and selfish appraisal of what's happening is just what I expect from you. I blame myself really. I think it's because you never settled down, had kids. You'd see things differently then, like I do.'

'Yeah, yeah, I've heard it before, but this is the way things are now. And I don't see anything wrong with the project at all. In fact, I'm quite enjoying my role in it. Despite my early reservations, remember them?'

'Yes, I remember, and maybe I should have

listened. But to be honest, son, I think you're only seeing the parts of the project you want to see. You're not seeing the misery it's causing elsewhere, the rampant damage, the destruction of habitats…'

'You're not going all "Greenpeace" on me are you, dad? You knew there would be changes when the ball was set in motion. You can't turn back the clock.'

'Well, actually I can.' The old man waved his hand in the air and the lights in the café dimmed until the two were sat in total darkness.

'Oh, dad, you're not going to say the words, are you? I'm having such fun.'

'Sorry son, something needs to be done to sort this mess out.' The old man paused, took a deep breath and then boomed 'Let there be Light.'

Flowers of the Field

'WHY HAVE YOU brought me all the way up here?'

'You'll find out soon enough,' was his gruff response.

Fleur isn't sure why she agreed to walk out with Jake that Sunday afternoon, after all, he was so much younger than her. She'd be nineteen in four months, and although only three weeks older than Jake, she lived a full school year in advance of him.

The age difference hadn't mattered before senior school. As close neighbours, they had fallen into an easy, natural friendship. In the village school the friendship continued, and they often explored local country lanes and moorland fells together.

This closeness all changed when Fleur went to secondary school. Overnight she became aloof. In the mornings, instead of walking to the village school with him, she left early and took the bus to the secondary school.

The following year, when Jake caught the bus out of the village, Fleur had a coterie of friends, and made it clear Jake would not be included.

Now it is May, and Fleur is sitting her A-levels and is expected to do well. In the autumn she will leave the village for university and, like many before her, will never return to live in the village again.

Jake had done well the previous year with his GCSE examinations, and is destined to study at university also, but in a different field. He knows that there will be little chance of him ever seeing Fleur again when the autumn comes. Yet through the long winter of his secondary school years he has carried a candle for Fleur. Jake took his courage in both hands and called to invite Fleur for a walk on the fells 'for old times' sake'. And Fleur, tired, worn and frustrated with being indoors for revision and exams, looked out at the bright, late spring afternoon, and agreed.

As they walked, and passed many of their old childhood haunts, Fleur gave a running commentary of the names, both English and Latin, of many of the plants that grew thereabouts. For Fleurs' interest was Botany, and she had used her early experiences well in making progress in her studies. But as they climbed above the valley in which their village nestled, these comments became fewer and fewer, until an awkward silence appeared between them. She filled it by asking Jake about his plans and interests. Jake explained his fascination with the night sky, and how this led to his study of physics and mathematics and his intention to study astronomy and cosmology at university.

Then the awkwardness fell between them again. Jake thought about how far apart they were. Not just in age, but in interests, hers on the ground and in the earth, his in the stars, and his heart despaired. Fleur thought about how little she really knew of Jake, her old childhood playmate talking about the origins of the universe.

They continued walking up the Fell, the awkward silence growing between them. Eventually Fleur could stand it no longer.

'Why have you brought me all the way up here?'

'You'll find out soon enough' was his gruff response.

Fleur was hot and becoming frustrated at the uncomfortableness between them.

'Look, I'm going home, it's getting too hot for me.'

'Hang on a couple of more minutes, Fleur, we're nearly there.'

'Nearly where?'

'Look, see that rocky outcrop, it's just by there.'

'Okay, okay, but what is it?'

'You'll see in a minute, I found it yesterday and immediately thought of you. I hope it's still there.'

'You mean this might all be for nothing; I should go now.'

'No, don't go, I'm sure it will be there. Look see this rock on the ground, I put it there as a marker. Come on!'

And with a childlike eagerness Jake unconsciously took Fleur by the hand. Not looking at her, but his eyes following a trail of small stones. Fleur gave him a quizzical look, but allowed herself to be drawn forward, noticing the strength in Jakes hand and arm, but also the gentleness with which he held hers.

Jake pulled her up the slope of the fell and then abruptly let go of her hand and fell to his knees, searching in the grass.

'It was definitely here yesterday'.

Curiosity got the better of Fleur and she slowly crouched down, until their heads were level.

'What was?' she asked, in an almost breathless whisper.

'There! Look!' he said as his hands gently parted the rough grasses of the limestone fellside to reveal the bright, turquoise blue flower of the tiny Spring Gentian, barely five centimetres tall.

She knew instantly what it was and gasped in amazement at this rarest of heathland flowers.

'Oh Jake! It's beautiful.'

'Well, I figure this is probably your last spring in Teesdale, and your last chance to see it. And what with you doing botany and all, I thought it would be a shame for you to go off never having seen the famous Blue Gentian'.

Slowly he took her hand and placed it on top of his own hand holding the grass aside from the blossom. Then he used his phone to take a photo of the flower and both their hands. He showed it to her.

'I could send it to you, if I knew your phone number, or email address,' he said quietly.

Fleur turned slowly to look at Jake. It felt like the first time she'd ever looked into his eyes, and she fell into them. Her breath left her as his arms wrapped around her.

The photo became wallpaper on Fleur's computer throughout her studies, and long after. Many people remarked on how lucky she was to have seen the flower, some even asked about the two hands in the photo. Sometimes she would say, sometimes not, but long after Jake ceased to be part of Fleur's life the photo remained.

Bonfire Night

THE BONFIRE HAD been built and the night was dark. Soon it would be time to set the flame. But before that could happen Jack would bring out the guy. The effigy he'd lovingly made with scrounged old clothes his mother was half glad to be rid of and stuffed with straw and old newspapers. The figure bulged and leaked through the torn trousers and the shirt with only half its buttons. But the mask was a delight. How Jack had manged to get a likeness of the miserable old couple across the road who always complained no matter what he did his parents would never know, but a likeness it was, combining both the tight lipped disapproving stare of the old woman and the discouraging shouts and piggy eyes of the old man.

Jack was about to run out of the back door with

the guy in his arms so his father could sit it atop the bonfire when the doorbell rang. His mother had just taken out some hot dogs for them and Jack was alone in the house. He crept through to the front of the house, which was in darkness and peered through the living room window. It was them. He quickly ducked down.

What now?

'Come on Jack, bring the Guy out. I'm freezing out here and want to get this fire lit.' It was Jack's father calling from the back garden. Jack left the guy and ran outside to explain.

'Mum, the people from across the road are at the door, they've rung the bell.'

'That's alright, pet, we're expecting them, go and let them in then bring that guy out.'

Expecting them! Jack couldn't believe his parents had invited the evil duo to his bonfire. What would they say if they saw the guy? He'd be in trouble again.

But Jack had to do what his mum said. He turned the Guy around as he passed through the kitchen to let them in.

'Hello Jack,' said Mrs Olden, 'bet you weren't expecting us today, were you?'

'No, I wasn't,' said Jack, trying to be polite but looking at anything but these unwelcome guests.

'Well, not to worry lad,' said Mr Olden, 'we'll not be here too long. Where's your father, I've something for him.'

That's when Jack noticed the bag he was carrying, it looked heavy with the handles being pulled tight in Mr Olden's hand. He took them through.

'That's a grand looking Guy, isn't it, Betty,' said Mr Olden.

'It is, very grand. Whoever made it certainly has an eye for detail.'

Jack picked up the Guy and the three joined his mum and dad in the garden.

'Mike, I've brought these along,' said Mr Olden.

'Fantastic,' said Jack's father, opening the bag. 'But I think you had better deal with these Geoff, you're the expert.'

Jack looked on in awe as Mr Olden pulled giant firework after giant firework from the bag.

'Here,' said Mrs Olden, 'if you're going to stand there with your mouth open, you'd better have this,' and she handed Jack the most enormous toffee apple he had ever seen.

It was strange after that night. Although the Oldens looked exactly the same to Jack, the Olden woman's stare seemed to be approving rather than disapproving, and the shouts of the old man seemed to positively encourage Jack in whatever he was doing.

The Minute

'I'll only be a minute' he said, 'I'm just popping out to get my Sunday paper'.

It's what he always said at this time on a Sunday morning. Every Sunday for thirty-four years George had 'popped out' for a minute to get a paper.

In the early years of their marriage he would run the three hundred metres to the newsagent, and then run back, so as not to miss a minute with his beautiful wife, and the newspaper would often end as a crumpled, forgotten ball in whatever room she happened to be in when he returned.

As time passed and their idyllic coupledom became populated by demanding children, he savoured the peace of the few minutes he was away and would sometimes take longer routes to the newsagent and back or stop to chat about nothings with half recognised neighbours along one of the streets.

Later still, as his children grew from babies and toddlers to grumpy, slovenly, bad-mannered teenagers, and he and his wife could not agree on how to 'deal' with them, he would call into the local pub after he had collected his newspaper. His return was either mellow and genial, or argumentative and bellicose, depending upon the company and his consumption of the local brew.

Latterly, since the children had left home, it was a pleasure to see someone else to talk to besides his wife.

Today, though, was different. Today was what he had been looking forward to and planning for seven years. Today he would collect his newspaper, but he would not be returning home. He had spent his whole life working and providing for his wife and family and had forgotten who he himself was. That was all going to change now. Today.

Since the two children had gone to live abroad, Australia and Canada, George and Susan never saw them from one year's end to the next. For ten years now the house had been populated only by the two of them. The conversations that they used to have gradually became arguments, and then turned to frosty silences. Less and less they spoke to each other of anything but the ordinary politeness's of the day.

It was after George had been made redundant from his firm in his mid-fifties that he had made the resolution and the plan. He could not, and would not, stay in the stifling, suburban atmosphere any longer than necessary. Gradually he filtered money from their joint savings accounts into a secret bank account of his own and began to explore where he might go. The travel section of the Sunday paper had previously been discarded unread but was now avidly consumed from cover to cover. Seven years later and he was ready.

As George left the newsagent he automatically turned and headed home, and he was halfway there and just about to turn the corner to their house when he realised what he had done. A black London taxi driving past him brought him to his senses and he remembered his plan. He turned and headed for the tube.

As it was Sunday, it took him a little longer to reach Heathrow than he had expected, but he was still in good time for the flight he had booked three months ago. That had been a particularly gruesome week, when George and Susan hardly passed a civil word, and hostility pervaded every room. The only bright part of the week was knowing that he had booked the flight, using money from his secret account. He delighted in the plan unfolding, and imagined the disappointment

Susan would feel after he had gone.

He had his passport in his pocket. That was interesting he thought to himself, making sure that he was the only one to see the several letters from the passport department that resulted in him finally getting the passport he needed, his first one. Poor Susan, she just had no idea. No idea about what was going on, no idea about George, and no idea about anything really.

As George entered the terminal building, an hour and a half after he had left home, he wondered if Susan had missed him yet. He wondered if she was thinking he'd gone to the pub again, something he had been doing sometimes lately, so she wouldn't get suspicious too early. No, she wouldn't be suspicious, she was too trusting to suspect him of something like this. Besides, if she was she would ring his mobile phone, and she would hear it ringing on the hall table where he had 'forgotten it' as he had done on a few Sundays lately. He smiled to himself as he pulled out his new, smart iPhone to check details of the flight. He also used it to check in online and avoided the queue of five or six at the check in desk.

George couldn't avoid the queue at airport security, however, and knew that it might take a while. He remembered queues in the past he and Susan had stood in, probably the most memorable was the huge queue for the concert that George had planned to take Susan to on their first proper date. They were going to see The Who at Hammersmith Apollo, and although they got there three hours before the doors opened there was already a huge queue. Three hours later there were six people ahead of them when the bouncers closed the doors. So instead of the concert they went to a local pub and spent the evening gazing into each other's eyes. They laughed about their one attempt to go to a proper gig many times in their early years together and told the story to their children until they themselves could recite it by heart.

On the other side of security George found himself a cup of coffee and headed for the departure lounge. Although this was a memorable day for him, George couldn't help but feel that the departure lounge was more like a railway station waiting room, than a precursor to a new life. He remembered the time when the four of them were stuck at a small railway station in Wales after a holiday. They had missed the train and had run out of money, but they played hide and seek and other games up and down the platform with the children. The lady who ran the kiosk took a shine to the children and gave them free ice creams, and a much-needed cup of tea to George and Susan.

It was while he was thinking of this that George's

flight was called to board. It took him a minute to realise that everybody nearby was getting up to catch the same flight, so he ended up at the back of the boarding queue. He looked about at the throng of close packed bodies trying to get through passport control first so they could get a good seat on the plane. He looked over the sea of unfriendly faces and felt strangely uncomfortable at the thought of sharing a tin can in the sky with them.

George turned and sat down with the few people who remained in the departure lounge. Some time passed, and he heard his name being called over the public address system. 'Last chance to board before the gates close,' the metallic voice said. He remained seated. An airport official walked among the seated travellers asking if they are George. When he is asked George hears himself say it is not him. The gates close. George hears the plane take off without him. He felt a profound sense of relief, and realised he must go home.

George retraced his steps through the airport, caught the tube, and as he passed the newsagent, he remembered he had left his newspaper in the airport. I'd better get another he thought, or she'll wonder where I've been. So George bought another newspaper and walked the three hundred metres home.

When George opened his front door, four hours after leaving, he decided not to say anything, she probably won't either he thought. He saw his phone on the hall table. There was a voice mail for him.

'Hi George, I'm glad you left your phone behind; it saves me writing a note. Just to let you know I can't stand it anymore and I'm leaving you. Don't try to find me, you won't. I've taken all the money. Got to go, I can hear the taxi arriving.'

Broken Resolve

It wasn't difficult. The first thing she did was convince him it was a good idea. And you know what men are like, brains in their gonads. A few subtle, or not so subtle suggestions, a couple of well placed, salacious words, hints at the promise of more, and they are slobbering to do your bidding. The hardest part is not to actually laugh out loud as they fall, yet again, for the oldest, and simplest, of subterfuges. It seemed such a simple idea. The flat needed decorating, he was a decorator. That she had no money, or no money she wanted to part with, seemed secondary at the time. He came round with his brushes and his paints, his ladders and his dust sheets, and set to work.

He was just finishing the kitchen when she realised it wasn't going to be that simple after all.

The unexpected ring at the door and him standing there with his sloppy sided grin and a bottle of cheap wine, suggesting they talk 'colour schemes', and she knew it would be a little more complex than originally thought. But hey, he wasn't so bad looking, and he'd had a shower, so what the heck, and besides, he'd done quite a decent job on the kitchen. So she opened a decent bottle of wine, and after they had finished that she opened the bottle he'd brought, and after they had finished that she opened her legs. The next day he started work on the next room.

As he was completing the bedroom, she knew he'd be round again, so she had a large gin and tonic beforehand. Sure enough, there he is, same bottle of cheap wine. 'I'll have to talk to him about wine' she thought to herself as she opened the bottle. This seems to be the tariff then, she thinks as he performs the old in-out on her, one shag per room. I can't say as he's really that good at it, she muses as he tidies himself before leaving.

The bathroom, the spare bedroom, the lounge, the hall, and then we'll be done. Thank God it's not a mansion, she thinks.

'No, really, it's not about that,' she says to him, 'it's been really good, but I'd like to do the hall myself, I fancy having a go and it's only a little room.', while she thinks, 'I just can't bear him to be near me, whatever possessed me to even think this might be a good idea.

So it's off to the hardware shop, tins of paint, brushes, all the stuff they try and sell you if you've never done the job before. You know, special brushes for the edges, special tape to cover switches and sockets, special this and special that. Stuff that sits in the cupboard until you move and then gets thrown away. Still, it's cheaper than paying someone she thinks, as she loads it into the car. Ah yes, the car, the old, battered banger someone gave her three years ago that, today, has decided it doesn't want to play anymore. 'How much?' she queries the garage call out man. 'Couldn't we come to an arrangement, you know, I'm sure there must be something we could do about the size of it, the bill I mean.' She says, with a girlish giggle. She showers immediately she gets in. For a long time. Still, it's money in the bank, she thinks to herself. And it was a very big bill.

'I'm not selling myself, it's not prostitution, it's more like, you know, friends with benefits.' She explains to her BFF over drinks one night. 'And I'd never do it with a plumber, that's such a porno cliché.' She gets home to find the boiler not working. It needs a new complicated and expensive part that he hasn't got with him but can bring round tomorrow. 'Oh good, that will give me chance to get to the bank' she thinks to herself, serious resolve at work. But the cost of a return flight to Athens! The money burns in her pocket as she considers and ponders. It won't take long she thinks.

The plumber arrives. He fixes the boiler. He gives her the bill.

'I was just going to take a shower to make sure it works,' she tells him. 'Why don't you come along? We'll see what we can do about that little bill.'

He laughs. 'I'm sorry, darling, you're lovely and all that, but I promised my wife there wouldn't be any more of that sort of thing. And I've already broken that resolution twice today.'

Persistence of Memory

I WAKE TO the sound of the sea. I have a bucket and spade, and a huge castle, complete with moat, to defend. I am the king of the castle and will repel all invaders, including the encroaching tide. I dig to maintain the sea defences. It is a losing battle, the moat fills and my castle is eaten away. I dig furiously. Then a helping hand, a strong, hairy arm, with another spade, joins me. The castle grows again. It's touch and go, but we have time for a breather. I look up from my labours and see my father smiling at me.

'A good castle you've built there, Kevin,' he says.

It's good to see him. 'Hello dad' I say, 'when did you get here'.

He pauses and thinks. I haven't seen him for three years, since I was six years old, since the day he fell off the roof, since the day he died. I feel tears in my eyes as he splutters unintelligible words and then vanishes in the space between sea and sand. The sea turns to nothing. It swirls about my feet. They are gone, and the rest of me follows.

I'm walking through the park on my way to meet a girl. Her names Julia and she's seventeen, like me. It's our first date. I'm taking her dancing. I see a figure crossing the park and think it might be her, but it's not. It's an old school pal. I recognise him. We greet each other. He walks beside me, and we chat.

Then he asks, 'are you going to meet Julia?'

I'm confused. He's never heard of Julia. I haven't seen him for three years. 'How come you know about Julia?' I say.

He pauses and begins to blur, like a camera out of focus, then shrinks to a point and is gone.

I walk on, it's dark now. I get to the park gate and step through into the black.

I am dancing. Julia is in my arms and we waltz around the room together. It's a competition and we are winning. We have trophies for our dancing. Julia keeps them all, her mother polishes them every week. We dance every Saturday and Wednesday, always with each other. Saturday's the best. It's then they have competitions. And it's when we might have a drink or two. I'll drink beer and Julia will have rum and coke. I'm going to marry her, if she'll have me. I will ask her tonight. I've got the ring in my coat pocket. She'll be excited, and I think she'll say yes. The music takes us away and we twirl round and round the dance hall. Everybody's clapping we must have won! I'll ask her now. I step into the cloakroom and I am lost.

I put the kids to bed while Julia gets changed. It's the first time we've been out by ourselves since our first was born. Now we have three.

'I'm so excited, Kevin,' says Julia, 'we haven't danced together for years.'

She's right, the couple of steps we can manage in the kitchen isn't dancing. The babysitter arrives, then our taxi to the Locarno Ballroom.

We dance every dance; I feel seventeen again. We have a drink or two, the band plays, the lights shine. It's the last waltz and I take Julia in my arms. We dance close, the glitter ball sweeps us along. When it's over Julia says she'll meet me outside. I say goodbye to friends then step through the door and there are only stars.

I've got my eyes closed. We're dancing cheek to cheek and I can smell your hair. I can smell half a century of dancing. I open my eyes to look at you.

Who's this? Who's this grey-haired old woman? 'I don't know you, you're not Julia, get away from me.'

Somebody says, 'are you all right Kevin? Is something the matter?'

I look. I know him. It's Jimmy, old Jimmy from the bowls club. What's he doing here? What am I doing here, in this draughty old hall? Where's Julia?

'Where is she,' I yell. I look around. Everybody is old. I'm old. I trip and fall through the cracks in the floor.

I sit in the best chair in the room. It's only right, I am the eldest. I have lost count of the years I've been here, on this planet, in this room, in this chair. They are eternal. People come, and they go. Some speak, others don't. Some do things to me, unspeakable things, things that hurt. I try to stop them, but I am weak. They tell me it's for my own good. What is good? Good is not this. Good is not this sitting. Good is not this sitting and being done to. Good is yesterday, good is when I was young. Good is dancing. I close my eyes. The light darkens to deep blue, thin-skinned eyelids not allowing darkness. I try to remember. I try to remember Julie, or Josephine, or was it Joleen, or…, or…, it doesn't matter, the name, I just try to remember her. Her face, so beautiful, so lovely like a…, like a…, oh, I don't know, like a beautiful thing. Her eyes so bright and, and blue? green? grey? I can't remember. It doesn't matter, they were, they were… eyes, that's what they were. Yes, eyes, those things you see with. I sing to myself, 'Jeepers creepers where d'you get those, those… those…' I sleep and slip and slide away. And all my memories follow.

How The Bland One Became Bunny

Miss Amelia Tulip did not have favourites amongst her class of seven-year-olds. She knew that would be unprofessional. But some made their mark on her, and she would relate tales of the classroom when having dinner with her new boyfriend, Danny. She tried to avoid the children's names, that would be unprofessional. Instead Amelia identified the subjects of her stories by their attributes. There was "the argumentative one", "the excitable one", "the stupid one", and "the clown". But none of these were the subject of her story that Saturday night, sitting opposite Danny in the restaurant he had suggested for their fifth date.

'Who will you tell me about tonight?' said Danny.

'Until yesterday I thought Benjamin, oops, shouldn't have said that, but I thought he was just the bland one. Not a huge intellect and little imagination. But a sweet kid. Or so I thought.'

'So what happened?' said Danny as he refilled Amelia's glass.

'I was shocked,' Amelia said, 'I felt myself blushing and had to quickly change the lesson plan.'

Danny was intrigued. He had said, and done, things which he was sure would raise a blush in the apple blossom features of his heart's desire, but she was imperturbable, dealing with his ardent advances as though he were a clumsy seven-year-old.

'What did he actually say?' said Danny.

'It was during "Show and Tell" time. You know, the kids all bring in whatever has taken their fancy and show it to everybody and say why they have brought it. "Benjamin, what have you brought in to show us" I ask all innocent, and he produces…' and at this point Amelia began to falter as her cheeks reddened at the memory.

'Go on,' said Danny, 'what did he show you?'

With a visible effort Amelia composed herself. She pulled her eyes from Danny's and closely studied the glass of red wine in her hand.

'He rummaged in his school bag and triumphantly produced a Rabbit,' she said.

'A live one?' asked Danny.

'No, Danny, not that sort of rabbit,' said Amelia. She was so intent on studying the glass of wine she didn't see Danny's bemused look and quizzical shake of his head. 'Then, with twenty-nine other seven-year-olds listening he said, "my mum says this is her best friend."'

'That kind of Rabbit!' said Danny, laughing.

'That's not all,' said Miss Tulip. 'The bland one had told his mother that I was his best friend so then he says "my mum said I bet your Miss Tulip would love to meet my best friend. So, I sneaked it out of the house so you could see if you wanted to be friends," and he held it out to me, pointy end first.'

'What did you do?' said Danny, eyes twinkling.

'He looked so proud of himself, but he couldn't have washed it,' said Amelia. 'I really didn't want to handle the thing. So I said, "That's alright Benjamin, I've got one of my own." Just as the head decided to walk in.'

Coffee

Mike sat at the table, turning the coffee cup on its saucer, occasionally taking a sip, peering up and down the street through the window. The café was empty apart from him. Monday mornings were never popular, he guessed. He looked at his watch; she was late. He wasn't surprised, she was often late. Apart from that one time when he'd assumed she'd be late so didn't arrive until ten minutes after the agreed time. There she was, incandescent with rage at his lateness. He's always been on time since then, but she never has.

'Do you want a refill?' It was the waiter, coffee jug in hand, smile on her face.

He looked at the dregs in his cup and glanced again at his watch. 'Thank you, I think I do.' He smiled back at her.

'It's always like this on Monday,' she said.

Mike looked at her name tag. 'Like what, Eve?'

'This quiet. Someone always comes in and I make a pot of coffee and then it just sits getting bitter so I try and give away as much as I can. I hope you don't mind.'

'No, I'm lucky, I guess. A free coffee.' And he smiled again.

'I'm going to have one myself, otherwise it'll just go down the drain,' said Eve. She returned to the counter and Mike heard the glug of coffee as he raised his cup and smelled his own. He glanced up and down the street again. She wasn't there. An involuntary sigh escaped him.

'Are you waiting for someone?' It was Eve, standing at his table again, this time holding her own coffee.

'She's late,' said Mike, 'she's always late.'

'I think that's ever so rude,' said Eve. 'If you make a plan you've got to stick to it, otherwise you're wasting people's time.'

Mike thought about how much time he'd spent waiting for Gabrielle in the six months he'd known her. It was too long.

'She must be something special though,' said Eve, moving her weight from one foot to the other.

"You can join me if you like,' said Mike.

'I'm not supposed to, the boss doesn't like it. But he's not here.' Eve pulled a chair out opposite Mike.

She was easy to talk to, open, honest, funny. Mike found his mood brightening, his anxiety about Gabrielle drifting away. He stopped peering out the window and watched Eve, her eyes, her mouth, that wisp of hair that had a will of its own. He stopped glancing at his watch but watched the subtle movements of Eve's body, her relaxed posture, her gestures as she spoke. Her lifting the cup to her mouth. He watched her throat as she swallowed, and he was beguiled.

Gabrielle chose that moment to walk in. The clang of the doorbell springing Eve to her feet and turning Mike beetroot.

Eve works at a different coffee shop now, in a different town, with Mike.

De-Cluttering

Even after I thought it finished, I found more to add.

Some were easy to find, laying in open view amongst the piles of other clutter common in twenty-first century lives. The first I collected would form the foundations, of the heap. Others needed rooting out from their hiding places. The loft, the spare room, even the garden shed.

I tracked them down over months, adding them to the pile.

Even after the certainty of no more settled on me I waited; remembering the odd cupboard I'd forgotten to search, or hidden boxes that held them. But I gathered them all up.

The bottom of the garden seemed the best place. It's where bonfires are usually built isn't it?

It grew slowly, took a long time to build. There

were many, many journeys up and down the garden, making sure every single one joined the pile. I was exhausted and it was dark by the time I'd finished.

'What are you doing?' said my patient and tolerant partner as we ate dinner.

'I'm having a bonfire. I'll be lighting it after dinner. It's quite big, should be seen for miles.'

'Sounds like fun,' she said.

I smiled my most genuine fake smile. 'You can watch if you like.'

November, the season of bonfires, hot and cold at the same time. We wrapped in coats before walking down together, carrying matches, the lawn mower petrol.

'Do you need this?' she said, nodding at the petrol can she carried.

'I want to make sure it gets going well.' Lies are easy when you've practised.

In the almost total darkness of the garden no one could see what the bonfire contained. No streetlighting illuminated its secrets, no torches shone on the heap. But the pile made its presence known in silhouette against a starry sky.

'It's huge,' she said.

'Yes, it's been a long time in the building,' I said.

I took the petrol can from her and walked around the heap, sloshing petrol as I went, until the can was empty.

'What's on it?' she said.

I struck a match and flicked it onto the heap of papers, diaries, folders, pads, and notebooks. 'Vanities,' I said as the flames began to roar.

The Coincidence

MICHAEL ENDURED THE clasp of the strong hand on his shoulder. He would have liked to have thrown it off in disgust, but he knew it belonged to Steve. And he admired Steve. Steve was tall, strong, handsome, popular, everything Michael wasn't. Steve acknowledging his presence was something at least.

'Hey Mike, a few of us are going to the pub after work. Are you coming?' said Steve, bonhomie oozing from every pore.

Michael hated being called Mike. His father had called him Mike and… well, just and. But in Steve's mouth Michael swallowed the hate and tried a smile. 'I'm not sure, will it be crowded?' Michael had refused every invitation during his three years in the office.

'Hope so,' said Steve. 'Angeline's coming.'

Angeline was the prettiest woman in the office. She and Steve had been flirting around each other for weeks. 'And she's bringing some friends.'

'I don't know. I'm not good in crowds,' said Michael.

'Suit yourself,' said Steve, his smile diminishing. 'It's a bit of a special do and you should be there, but nobody can make you.'

Steve wandered away and Michael returned to the boring, tedious, repetitive work he excelled at. It suited his personality.

During the morning break most of the staff gathered together for coffee. Michael took the opportunity to continue being alone and remained at his desk reading.

Crying from across the room alerted him to the presence of someone else in the office. He couldn't see, but there were two women, one crying the other making soothing noises. Michael slumped further down in his chair.

'Why is he so horrible?' said the crying one through her tears. Michael recognised the voice of Catherine, a young quiet woman who worked in a pod on the other side of the office.

'To be honest,' said the other girl Michael recognised as Angeline, 'he's only speaking the truth. You are pretty dowdy and never join in the fun stuff.'

Catherine resumed wailing.

'And another thing, I'll not be bothering with you anymore if you can't just join in for one evening. You are pretty pathetic. Maybe you should think about that.' Michael heard Angeline leave the office. Only Catherine's sobs filled the room.

Poor Catherine. She never hurt anyone, she was always quiet and polite. Michael tried to stand and go to her, but his heart started pounding and he began to sweat. What would he say? But everyone would be back soon, and Catherine still sobbed.

He stood and stumbled across the office to her cubicle. Her head was on her desk, her hands over her head.

'I'm not going either,' he said.

She startled out of her sobs and sat up. 'I didn't know anyone was here,' she said. 'I'm always the only one in here at break time.'

'I thought I was. I can't stand noisy crowds. How did you annoy Angeline so much?'

'I only said I was going to the library after work and couldn't go to the pub.'

'That's a coincidence,' said Michael. 'I'm going to the library too.'

Out with the Old

'LIKE A PHOENIX from the ashes, you mean?'

'Well not exactly, but it works as a metaphor.'

'You'll be completely changed?'

'Sort of, parts of me, maybe. Some of me definitely. They say.'

'Whose they?'

'The experts doing this. They said, "if you want a new you for a new year just come along and we can fix it for you." Out with the old and in with the new.'

'Yeah, okay, but what does all that mean.'

'It means I'll be completely different, a new person, you won't recognise me.'

'You're kidding. I'm your best mate, of course I'll recognise you.'

'I'm telling you, I'll be unrecognisable, even to you.'

'You're not doing this just because it's your turn to buy the beer are you? It seems a bit extreme to avoid a round.'

'No, I promise to buy the beer. I'll even meet you in the pub after it's all over, but you won't know who it is buying your pint. I'm telling you; these guys are fantastic.'

Do you know anyone who's had it done already, this, what does it say on the leaflet... this transmogrification, whatever that is?'

'I do, as it happens. A bloke at work had it done before Christmas. That caused a stir at the office party, I can tell you. Security almost threw him out, saying his ID was clearly faked.'

'It's pretty extreme then.'

'I think that's an understatement.'

'And it's expensive I guess.'

'It's not cheap. But then if was cheap it'd be crap wouldn't it. Who wants to be transmogrified into a piece of sh...'

'Well, no one, of course. I was just wondering if I could afford it.'

'You can't just wander in and be changed like that, you know. You've got to make an appointment, and they're hard to come by. It seems a lot of people want to metamorphose these days.'

'I think I'll probably wait to see how it turns out for you. I'm always a bit wary of these latest ideas.'

'You've never been an "early adopter" have

you? It was years before you got a decent phone.'

'I'm just careful, that's all. I'll just wait and see how it pans out for you. When is your appointment?'

'Saturday. It was more expensive for the weekend, but I didn't want to take time off work. And I wanted to get used to it before going back in. I'll meet you in the pub Saturday night if you like, buy you that pint.'

'Will you be okay, going out so soon after?'

'They said I should be, if everything went to plan.'

'Okay then, I'll see you then.'

'You drinking bitter then?'

'Blimey, you were right, I didn't recognise you.'

'What do you think then? Quite a change, eh?'

'It sure is, I've never seen anything like it. Where is this place again?'

'It's down McAllister Avenue, behind the market place. Are you going to try them?'

'No, I just want to make sure I get my haircut anywhere else.'

The Target

THE TARGET WASN'T difficult to find. Probably the easiest in my career with an organisation that would not appreciate being named. And that career spans decades and hundreds of targets. I've had only one failure. The target wasn't killed, my shot was inaccurate. But paralysis from the neck down was sufficient for my employers to allow me another opportunity. That was many years ago, but the lesson remains with me. I always ensure the target does not survive.

Some of my targets have been prominent people. Easy to find but hard to get close to and get away. Others have been shadowy figures, tough to unearth, suspicious and dangerous. Those are the hardest. Always it's a matter of risk reduction. Slowly get them accustomed to your existence, allow them to think you're unimportant, but useful, let them learn not exactly to trust you but to drop their guard just enough. Never take the first opportunity, it's usually a test. Take your time and allow them to feel just a little comfortable. Do it during something routine and mundane.

I take longer over my work than most in this sphere, and charge more for my services. But I also live longer. But it's not the money that keeps me working, taking assignments, finding targets, executing them. The real reason is sheer enjoyment. I love the hunt, the deception and, finally, the killing.

I've watched this target for a long time. It's a woman, but many of my targets have been women. I know her routine, where she goes during the day, who her friends are, what she eats, when she sleeps.

So here I am, the Glock in my gloved hand, the silencer fixed, the safety off, and the target unconscious. Don't misunderstand. I haven't knocked her out, she's merely sleeping, totally unaware of my presence in the room. It is dark. I see by the dim red light of a torch I wear on my head. I'm dressed in the assassin's uniform of black, with soft, squeak free shoes. I hold the gun, it's barrel only an inch from the target's temple, my finger on the trigger.

And I hesitate.

I pull the gun away, click on the safety catch,

unscrew the silencer, and slip the Glock into its shoulder holster. There's going to be trouble with my employer, I know. But I'm already scheming how to deal with those who will give the orders as I shake the target awake.

'We need to talk,' I say to my daughter as she opens her eyes.

Back to School

You're walking slowly this morning. This evening you'll be walking quickly, might even be running, but probably not, probably just a quick walk. But this morning it's a slow walk, a long and slow walk, savouring every minute of the time you have not being there. You don't need to say where, we already know.

You have done this walk many times. Like those other times, you find it easy to be distracted on this bright early autumn day, easy to find much of interest anywhere on the familiar route. You discover yourself fascinated by insects on the ground, birds in the air, other people doing the same, slow walk as you. You even find Mrs Barraclough's new net curtains interesting, but just like the old ones, they have that constant twitch of the ever-present owner, desperate to witness some misdemeanour on which she can vent her otherwise unexpressed frustrations. You hope you are not present when it happens, you usually manage to avoid her, and your pace quickens ever so slightly at the thought that she may target you.

Soon you are past her, but that means you are close to the destination and there at the end of the road they loom, the school gates. You try and keep your spirits, try to keep hold of some of the summer, some of the joy of the last six weeks without the hustle of daily school. But you know that when you step in those gates another school year will begin and your heart sinks. Part of you seriously contemplates not going in, running away, turning your back on it, but you know you won't do this, the repercussions would be painful and long lasting. So with your heart, now getting heavier at every slow step, you cross the threshold into school territory once again.

The cacophony of voices pummels you as you make your way across the tarmac to the door. Voices call out to you, some call your name, some hurl insults, but none of them is individually identifiable. It's always like this on the most hateful day of the school term. You fix a plastic smile across your face and nod to both right and left as you scurry across the playground, your stride now urgent, yet careful, to avoid the gobbets of spit and chewing gum that lie in your path.

You grab the handle of the door and immediately regret it. What monster has left this abominable stickiness beneath your hand. You step inside and are met by your nemesis, by the horror you have pushed your mind away from facing for six long weeks. A face looms at you. It is the person who insists on your attention, who makes every excuse to intrude on you, the dour and domineering school secretary, Miss Lonelyheart.

'Welcome back,' she says, 'I'm so pleased to see you again, I've missed you all summer, headmaster.'

You think she may be smiling, but it's hard to tell.

Gardening is for Life

GARDENING HAS ALWAYS been a pleasure. An act of creation and optimism. An investment in the future. A garden will provide a healthy diet, a space for contemplation, a frisson of excitement as the year begins its creative beat and buds begin to swell and open.

Yes, you could say I like gardening, I suppose you could even say I love my garden. But it is a hard taskmaster. It doesn't yield its fruits easily to the untrained hand and requires constancy if it is to be at its best.

So, with fork and spade and trowel and hoe I tamed the garden, bent its will from wildness to productivity and orderly beauty.

But, as you know, I've never really been that keen on the 'orderly beauty' side of stuff. I'm much more a fruit and veg man myself. Picking and eating the fruits of my own labour, that's what I love. You always knew that. I don't mind mowing the lawn every so often or trimming the hedges. These always need doing. But it's the whole choosing and placing flowers and shrubs stuff I can't be bothering with. I know when and where to plant leeks, onions, broccoli, carrots. These are useful, I can eat them. But flowers, with all those Latin names, they just don't inspire me.

So, I hope you don't mind, but I've decided to just concentrate on veg. It's a fertile plot and should crop abundantly for a long time. This time of year, it's early rocket, spring onions and a few radishes, hopefully to produce a few nibbles as the sun warms up. It's a good spot for a garden. It's not too shaded so seeds should germinate and grow away well. I might use one of those glass bell jars if it looks like being really cold. That would look good. You'd like that.

Afterwards I'll put some beetroot in. You've always loved beetroot. I'll bring the plants on first, so they are ready as the early salad comes out. Then in June some of your favourite French beans. When the frosts come, later in the year, I'll make sure I've got a few leeks in. They'll keep me coming back over the winter.

I shan't grow any parsnips though. Even though we both like them. They're a bit too deep rooted for this plot. I couldn't go digging them up in the middle of winter could I. Especially not if they are like some of my prize winners, more than two feet long.

As you know I like to share my produce with friends and neighbours. But I think you'd like me to keep what grows here for me. I shan't share anything growing in this little plot, not even with the Sexton.

Nightlife

I HATE IT at this time of year. It's cold, it's wet, it's windy, it's horrible.

It would be okay if it were summer, I don't mind it then, warm nights, balmy southerly breezes, but the nights are so short. There isn't time to get everything done, so no time to enjoy myself.

But in the winter the nights are long, and so are the working hours. I hate it. Better get going though.

First up it's old Mrs Marjory Strumple. She'll be early to bed. Although she's a Mrs it's been many tears since old Eric Strumple passed away. Every night she wakes up thinking she can hear him, and who am I to disappoint the old lady. I don't expect I'll be doing this particular job many more years, she's pretty rickety, but still, got to be diligent. I think a little 'woooing' down the chimney should do the trick for her. Yep, there she is, I can feel her heart rate rising and she's beginning to tremble in bed. 'Is that you Eric, is it?' she calls out. It's the same every night, and he never answers of course. I give her a last fading 'wooo' and move on.

Now it's on to the young couple in their new house. Their first ever home they can call their own. It's stressful is moving, and they've been arguing like couples sometimes do. But they've made up in the time-honoured fashion and he thinks everything is fine now. I use his voice and I whisper in her ear, 'I'll always love you, Julie'. She's awake in a flash. 'Who's Julie, you bastard,' she yells as she thumps him awake. I cackle to myself and move on.

And so it goes through the long, lonely night. From house to house I go, scaring the innocent, the believers and unbelievers alike. Making dogs bark, soot fall. Scratchings in the roof space, the knock at the door with no one there, strange lights, with no source, all waking people in the dead of night. They're just the common ones. Countless are the ways of haunting, and looking about I suspect that you all know that, you've all experienced it at least once. That's why I'm so busy. Especially in the winter when the nights are long, and the cold is deep.

But it's getting late and my work for the night is almost done. I've one more call to make before returning to the graveyard. And I guess, if you haven't heard me already tonight, you'll know where I'll be heading.

The Miller's Wife

THIS STORY WAS inspired by a visit to Sturminster Newton Mill on the banks of the river Stour in Dorset. The weir was washed away in a flood and the miller's cottage was demolished to repair it. Although these events took place in the nineteen twenties the story is set at an earlier date. There has been a mill on this site since before the Domesday Book was compiled. There are photos of the cottage and of the weir being repaired in the guidebook to the mill. The author strongly recommends a trip to the mill for an insight into the lives of ordinary people in the past. The guided tour is excellent.

Sarah, the miller's wife, looked on with a growing sense of unease as the men worked. She hid her anger and busied herself attending to the men's needs for food and drink. She tried to subdue her feelings, but it was hard.

She understood the reasons it was happening,

but that didn't mean she was happy about it. Peter, the miller, had taken the time to explain it in great detail.

'It's not just about you and me', he said, ''tis about all the folks hereabouts. Where are they to get their flour if the mill's not working? And how are the womenfolk going to feed their men and children without bread?'

Sarah understood that these questions from her husband were not intended for an answer but were explanations of why he was doing what he was doing. She understood that the work had to be done. People would starve without bread, and it would be the poor people who starved first. Her brothers and sisters and their families amongst them.

Even so, Sarah had argued.

'Isn't there some other way?' she said, 'can't you find what you need somewhere else nearby?'

Although Peter had learned to be patient with his wife over the years they had been together, for he loved her dearly, he also felt the pressure of time upon him and knew that if he delayed his actions things would only get worse.

'I've explained it the best I can,' he said, 'If that's not good enough then so be it. It's the only way we can get the mill working again, and there is nowhere hereabouts with the amount of stone we need that is so handy.'

'Handy is it! That's what it's become, handy!' Sarah could not help letting her anger get the better of her, but inside she knew he was right.

'Look at the track Sarah,' said Peter, 'even if we had the stone nearby it would take an age to get it here. The flood's taken the track away and left a bog. It will be days until it's dried out, and by then folks will be needing flour and the track will be full of grain carts.'

So the men worked. They worked hard and all day to rebuild the weir. The weir that had been washed away in one of the highest and fastest floods anyone could recall. The weir that held the mill pond that provided the head of water to turn the mill wheels. The weir that fed all the families in Sturminster parish.

The stone they needed to rebuild the weir came from the only place available. From the cottage that Sarah called home. The cottage she had cared for all the years of her marriage. The cottage over which threshold her husband had carried her on their wedding day. The cottage where her sons and daughters were born.

Stone by stone, row by row, the cottage shrank and the weir grew. Finally the weir was repaired and held firm against push of the water. But of the cottage not a stone remained.

Nightmare

There was an insisting rapping at the window. Who could it be? It wasn't so much late at night as early in the morning, and I can just see the grey of dawn pushing through the curtains.

I look at the bedside clock and groan. Four forty-five. Not even five o'clock. Who the devil is it? The rapping sounds again. A knuckle beating on the window. Why did I take the lease on this ground floor flat? I lurch out of bed, pull on some pants and make for the window. I pull the curtain aside just in time to see a slim figure leaving hurriedly through the gate. I stare, surely it can't be my sister. Yet from behind it looks like her. I must be mistaken; Tamsin is in New York. She's just got a job with a hot shot fashion mag over there and she's loving it. What's she doing here? It can't be her. As I turn to go back to bed and hopefully to sleep, I hear a cry and look again. There is no mistaking her this time as she turns her head and looks right in my eye. 'Nick, Nick come, quick!' she calls, a note of distress in her voice. I know it's her. That unmistakeable curl of hair over her right eye. The very image of that over my own, except that Tammy makes a feature of hers and I try to hide mine. There she is calling me to go to her. Then I watch as she is pulled through the gate by someone, or something, unseen. I grab a shirt and my jacket and leave the flat. Quickly down the three paces to the front door and out into the garden. There's no sign of her. I hear her calling me again. 'Nick, please come quickly', her voice almost sounding like my own when I get into an argument. We share many things, my sister and me. She's just round the corner I'm sure of it. I sprint as I pull my j acket on, but as I turn the corner there is no one to be seen. A quiet leafy street in a quiet leafy suburb. I'm too awake to go back to bed so I walk to the main road where I know there is a café that opens early and decide to treat myself to coffee and bacon rolls for an early breakfast before going home to change for work.

It's almost six o'clock when I order my second coffee. My phone rings. It's Tamsin. It's two am in New York. I take the call and before I can speak she says, 'Nick, are you OK, I've just had a terrible nightmare!'

'Hi Tammy' I say, even though I know she hates being called Tammy now she's in New York, not sophisticated enough. 'You've had a terrible nightmare, so have I, and about you, and that's why I'm sat in this coffee bar at six am drinking second rate coffee instead of being all nicely tucked up in the land of nod'.

I'm surprised she doesn't take the 'Tammy' bait; she normally does. Instead she says 'I'm so relieved to hear your voice, look, whatever you do don't go…'

It's then I hear the low 'crump' of an explosion in the distance, and the signal is cut.

My flat, and the rest of the house, was totalled in the explosion. The occupants of the other eight flats were all killed. For a while I was under suspicion, not being able to really say why I had left the building suddenly, but that ended when the fault in the gas main came to light.

But hey, sisters eh, who'd be without one.

What I Did on my Holidays

It was a glassy eyed stare that met the class on the first lesson every Monday. Mainly because the English teacher, "Killer" Rodley, famously had a glass eye.

The pupils of Form 2B, myself included, were never sure which eye was glass and which was real. Killer seemed able to see equally well out of both eyes when there was mischief in the classroom. And on Monday mornings after a school holiday, whether six weeks in summer or a scant few days in freezing February, it would be the same.

'Write at least two pages about, "What I did on my holidays", you have forty minutes, and complete silence is required.'

The groan from the class on each of these occasions was necessarily silent. Mr Rodley's nickname was well earned, and every term he looked for an opportunity to enhance his reputation. Those who lifted their heads from their writing were met with Killer's baleful glare, and nobody dared to meet that look more than once.

We found the exercise almost impossible. The likelihood of any of us having been on holiday was less than slim. Time not at school was spent in the park or on the streets, and invariably involved football. The beautiful game was a subject as distant from Mr Rodley's interest as the beaches of Cannes and Monaco were from the northern council estate we called home. The fate of a boy who had written about football had become legend in the school, and none of our juvenile scribbling risked the subject.

Apart from football, Mr Rodley did not care what we wrote about. Attempts to find family events significant enough to fulfill the assignment quickly gave way to imagination. It became a playground competition to see who could spin the most outlandish stories.

I had completely forgotten Mr Rodley and his exercises until years later. I happened to be staying in Wells, a pretty little town in Somerset. I was mooching around when I saw it, filling the window of Waterstones, "What I did on my Holidays – Vol 8, Book Signing Today". I had to have a look, so stepped inside. The book was a collection of short stories. I skimmed a couple then one caught my eye. It felt familiar, I knew what it was about. Names and locations had been altered and the writing was no longer that of a twelve-year-old, but it was one of my own schoolboy stories. I looked at the authors name, "Rocky Kidler", it was just too close.

There was a queue of half a dozen people or so waiting to have copies signed; and at the end of the queue there he was at the desk, older, of course. As I waited in line I recalled that I never witnessed Killer Rodley meting out the summary justice he was legendary for, never saw him punish a fellow pupil. He ruled us by reputation alone. When my turn came he took my book and opened it to the title page.

'Who should I dedicate it to?' he said.

'Make it out to Turner, Form 2B,' I said.

He looked at me. 'Ah yes, Turner, I recognise you.' He held my gaze for a few seconds. I still couldn't tell which eye was real.

He gave a little half smile as he watched my eyes flick from one to another of his. 'You were always one of the more imaginative ones,' he said. He dedicated it to "The imaginative Turner, Form 2B", then he drew a cartoon eye and wrote, "Could be either, or neither". He handed it back to me and said, 'Now you know what I did on my holidays.'

About the Author

Rik Lonsdale's lifelong desire to write had been held in check through three previous careers and the raising of children. Eventually he was able to turn his energies to learning the art and craft of writing.

Water and Blood, his first novel published in March 2023, was inspired by his concern for the future of civilisation and the human race.

Morsels of Life, his first collection of short stories, shares his love of people, their humour, and humanity.

Rik lives in Dorset, UK. When he isn't writing you can probably find him at the bottom of his garden tending his vegetable plot.

If you would like to know more about Rik and his writing journey you can find him at www.riklonsdale.com or on social media.

If you enjoyed 'Morsels of Life' you can let the author know through his website, via social media, or by writing a review.

www.ingramcontent.com/pod-product-compliance
Lightning Source LLC
Chambersburg PA
CBHW032225190726

48289CB00007BA/2397